WHAT HAPPENS IN VEGAS
WILL NOT STAY IN VEGAS

WHAT HAPPENS IN VEGAS WILL NOT STAY IN VEGAS

ZSAZSA K. LOUIS

WHAT HAPPENS IN VEGAS WILL NOT STAY IN VEGAS

iUniverse books may be ordered through booksellers or by contacting:

iUniverse
1663 Liberty Drive
Bloomington, IN 47403
www.iuniverse.com
1-800-Authors (1-800-288-4677)

Because of the dynamic nature of the Internet, any web addresses or links contained in this book may have changed since publication and may no longer be valid. The views expressed in this work are solely those of the author and do not necessarily reflect the views of the publisher, and the publisher hereby disclaims any responsibility for them.

Any people depicted in stock imagery provided by Thinkstock are models, and such images are being used for illustrative purposes only. Certain stock imagery © Thinkstock.

ISBN: 978-1-5320-0833-7 (sc)
ISBN: 978-1-5320-0835-1 (hc)
ISBN: 978-1-5320-0834-4 (e)

Library of Congress Control Number: 2016915967

Print information available on the last page.

iUniverse rev. date: 09/29/2016

To my friends and family, who have helped
me and encouraged me along the way

CONTENTS

CONTENTS

AUTHOR'S NOTE

It has been about 250 years since François-Marie Arouet, who is better known by his nom de plume of Voltaire, first published his great work *Candide*. The book tells the story of a young man, Candide, who has been living a sheltered life. In his home, Candide is regularly indoctrinated to see life only through rose-colored glasses.

The book then describes the abrupt cessation of this lifestyle, followed by Candide's disillusionment as he witnesses and experiences great hardships and tragedies in his travels around the world. Voltaire concludes the story of Candide by advocating a practical outlook on life in order to be truly content: "We must cultivate our garden!"

While there has been some disagreement over the meaning of Voltaire's advice, I prefer to think that Voltaire meant that all of us should strive to improve things through our own efforts in our own environments. In the words of John Donne, "no man is an island entire of itself; every man is a piece of the continent, a part of the main …"

In my case, I was born in Budapest, Hungary, where I worked as an attorney and lived a sheltered existence for a large part of my life, under a Communist regime that tried to convince the population that there was no better way to live. Once I left Hungary, I embarked on a series of adventures and misadventures, many of which happened in Las Vegas and many of which are included in this book in the form of essays and short stories.

Yet I believe that it does not matter where we come from; it only matters where we are headed and whether we have a clear eye along the way no matter what adventure or misadventure we face. Because, in the end, we will always prevail with love, determination, and goodwill to others, no matter the odds. To that end, I hope that these essays and short stories will not only prove to be a fascinating look behind the curtain but also share some helpful information about life in Las Vegas or anywhere that humans may be engaged in some folly.

It is goodwill toward others that can make our lives better and give purpose to our days. We were not made for our own selves— we can be happy only if we try to serve others and try our best to be good to others. My story ends with me finally finding a new life as part of the American continent, meeting many nice people along the way, to whom I owe a world of gratitude for their help and, in some cases, inspiration for these stories.

Finally, and most importantly, I would like to say a special thanks to my son, who edited my work; to David Lednitzky, who prepared my cover art; to my friends; and to my manager, Adam Beza—all of whom patiently read my many rough drafts and encouraged me to finish this project. Most of all, I want to give thanks to God for giving me the strength to undertake this difficult endeavor.

CHAPTER 1

THE GAME

We humans like to play games. We enjoy solving puzzles. We sometimes even enjoy the thrill of risk. All of that and more is available in Las Vegas, Nevada. While gambling is the main attraction, the town has hotels, shows, and many other amenities. Las Vegas is an exciting city—the gaming and entertainment capital of the world. While there are many beautiful and shiny casinos in this town, below the surface there are many hidden tragedies, which are kept hidden to avoid negative publicity for the city and the casino industry.

There are, of course, different games that individuals play in real life: political games, social games, sports, and gambling games. Gambling games are kind of guessing games that unfold in accordance with strict rules and have outcomes that are not always understood. Yet casinos make people responsible for their gambling.

Indeed, in this gambling paradise, rookies are always welcome. When those who are rookies in gambling begin to play, they do not, of course, know much about gambling. Often they keep losing. In the end, they become wiser in the ways of gambling as a result of their negative experiences. However, these rookies do not represent any substantial risk for the Las Vegas casinos.

On the other hand, there are also many professional gamblers, who are a much higher risk for casinos. These players know how to face off with the casinos, as they are good at using proper strategy as well as different tricks. For example, card counting in blackjack is an efficient way of having information on how to properly bet. Of course, the casinos do not allow it and exclude players who are suspected of card counting. Most of these professionals have an addiction and believe that they will win big-time. Yet they will still lose in the end because the odds of the game are ultimately against them.

There are also many who are merely spectators of the games— who visit the casino just to watch the action, to listen to the live music, to get free drinks. Some of them will sit down only briefly at the card tables to get their free drinks. Others will stay longer and act as cheerleaders for the other players at the gambling table. Sometimes they behave the worst to staff, because they do not have anything to lose. Sometimes they even try to run the table game, notwithstanding the presence of the table-game dealer, who is required by the casino to be in charge.

Casino table-game dealers are on the front lines, and they have to provide good customer service while the guests of the casino are gambling at their tables. That is not an easy job.

I have been a table-game dealer in one of the best casinos for a long time. I also worked in other casinos in the past. During my daily work, I had many opportunities to observe people's behavior, both when they had some good luck and also when they had bad luck.

In my line of work as a table-game dealer, we are regularly faced with unknown people and situations as an integral part of our job. As a result, we have many unexpected daily surprises, and as such, we have to stay flexible, calm, and alert at all times. To be a dealer is an all-consuming job that requires a lot of endurance and people skills. It is especially difficult to exercise proper people skills when someone has just lost a lot of money and is understandably mad and wants to pick a fight. Even if a player is otherwise doing well, interpersonal situations at a gambling table can get very tricky.

One day, I dealt at the three-card poker table on the casino floor, and it happened that a customer got six cards in his hand because he had also grabbed his son's three cards from the table. I was initially unaware that this was happening. At this time, I was in the middle of explaining the rules of the game to another player, who was also seated at my table in the first base position.

However, when I recognized that the player seated at the other end of the table was now holding six cards, instead of the permitted three cards, I had to act.

"Wow, I need another set of eyes to see what is going on here. You know, it is not proper to play three-card poker with six cards in any casino," I said.

"My father got confused and mistakenly also picked up my dropped cards," responded the son of the player who was holding the six cards.

Indeed, the player with six cards was very old. The table-game supervisor, who then approached, understood the situation. As a result, the old man did not get escorted from the casino. Only I had to recover from a sense of initial panic because table-game dealers are responsible for all the activity at their tables, even if it is none of their doing. Earlier that evening, I had had problems with some other inexperienced players.

"Sorry, but we are rookies," they told me after the supervisor let them off.

"It is okay; we all have to learn sometimes," I told them.

However, even if the player is inexperienced, if something goes wrong, the casino still makes it the dealer's responsibility. In fact, almost everything that happens at the table is held against the dealer both by management and by the players. It is also a little bit like being a flight attendant on a plane—while the public perception is that you are there for customers' service and entertainment, the reality is that your primary responsibilities are proper and efficient performance, loss prevention, and public safety.

At another time, I was dealing cards at the blackjack table, and one of the players tried to double down on his hand after he'd already received three cards. However, to double down, the player has to do so with his initial two-card hand. It would not have been that bad, but after I needed to correct him, the player kept insisting for the next two hours that he was right and that I was wrong.

Later, another player tried to split a seven and an eight.

"The casino will only let you split same-value cards," I told him. This was, in fact, the universal rule in all Las Vegas casinos and, to my knowledge, in all casinos around the world.

"At home in Idaho, we split any cards," he responded.

"The casino has its house rules, which players have to follow. However, no harm done; you are welcome to split another hand," I responded.

I remember thinking to myself that I was surrounded by experts! More seriously, the daily training and policing of the players falls on the table-game dealers. Guests arrive daily with great ideas on how to win. They feel that the casino's rules and the dealers are only in their way. Therefore, they try to manipulate the game. They want to play the game in accordance with their own made-up rules and not in accordance with the standard rules. It is a bit like playing any board game with a small child. Dare to win, and the child will claim that you were cheating and you need to change the rules.

Given this mind-set, the patrons, who are probably law-abiding and good neighbors in their own hometowns, will regularly act against the regulations of the casino and will otherwise engage in psychological warfare with the table-game dealers. Changing a bet after the first card is already out or putting up big stocks of different-colored chips with fifty cents on top are regular occurrences. To further undermine the dealer's ability to concentrate, many players will intentionally blow smoke directly into the table-game dealer's face or find other intentional ways of irritating the dealer. Such methods are well known in the industry. All table-game dealers suffer silently under such treatment.

"We do not want you to feel too comfortable," a player once told me.

Another common tactic in blackjack is that a player will not give the proper hand signals, or otherwise play irregularly, in order to make the dealer "break the hand," rendering the dealer unable to properly complete a single cycle of cards dealt within a portion of the game. Often the rules and probabilities of the game will be completely ignored with incongruent betting.

Sadly, players will many times use very foul language, cursing with great frequency. Sometimes some will even pound the table loudly.

"It is my money; I will play it the way I like it" is the refrain that is often heard from players.

"Yes, you're right; however, it is to be played by our rules" is my required response.

Recently, one of the players at the crazy-four poker table played a blind hand. This means that he is not allowed to look at his cards. Notwithstanding, he did pick up his cards a few times.

"Sir, it is against the rules to look at your cards if you play blind," I had to advise him in accordance with the house rules.

"Do not try to be smart. That is my money, and the rules are written on the table," he retorted.

"The rules on the table are the payment rules," I responded, and then I further clarified the obvious: that a blind hand means you cannot peek at your cards. In the end, I needed to call my table-game supervisor to explain the casino rules for the game. Clearly in some cases, the rules are unfamiliar, but in many others, the patrons just want to bend the rules.

One of the most popular table games in the casinos is still blackjack. However, not all patrons know or even care to follow the rules of this classic game either. In my experience, almost all the players know a little bit about its rules, and some others know more but wish to confuse the dealer, and there are many who are just too inebriated to care.

In most cases, most of the individuals walk into a casino thinking that they will win all the money that day that is played at the table. In the end, they lose everything because the statistical probabilities of the games favor the house. In fact, in looking at the underlying math, casinos really win (make their money) not when a player loses; they make their money when the player wins.

This sounds counterintuitive, but it is true. At any moment, the casino is engaged in hundreds of betting transactions. It is inevitable that it will win some of the time and lose at other times. However, paying a player less than in proportion to the risk that the player assumed in making a bet assures continued profitability for the house. For example, when a player places a bet on any number on roulette, his or her odds of losing that bet are thirty-eight to one, yet the winning hand is paid only thirty-five to one by the casino.

The gambling palaces in Las Vegas are a testament to the fact that the odds favor the house.

Correctly, casinos advertise responsible gambling, which means that gamblers have to be at least twenty-one years old and have to decide at the beginning of the games how much they will spend and when they will stop. It is their money that will be at risk. It is their responsibility to stop.

While players have to be twenty-one years old or older, many of them are not and try to use fake identification. Some underage young men come into the gambling space wearing baseball caps and sunglasses in an attempt to mask their true age.

A lot of players are not familiar with the casino's system and environment at all. Even if they are familiar with the odds, the casino, and the rules of the games, the free flow of alcohol, the high level of disorienting noise (both visual and auditory), the sense of timelessness, and the disorienting spatial relations—all of which are intentional by design—still raise doubts about whether certain decisions are made rationally.

In fact, an environment filled with loud music, loud signs, free drinks, lack of straight lines to the casino's exits, and missing clocks can create a disorienting effect on the mind. Such a milieu, which is often combined with a patron's lack of knowledge of the games and true odds, ensures that most players lose most of their money most of the time. In this environment, even a rational human being is not fit to make the right decision, and therefore, some of them will even play until their last penny.

"Where is the exit? I feel completely lost," I am often asked.

"Often I feel lost too," I sometimes respond when I show the direction to the nearest exit.

One weekend, a group of men returned from their convention to their hotel and decided to spend some time in the casino at the blackjack table to which I was assigned. I felt fortunate to be in their company, because they were polite and had a good sense of humor, even when they were losing. They made me laugh.

"Do not get fresh with the dealer, buddy, because she will beat you like a ragged donkey," said one of them to his friend, following a compliment that his friend had paid to me.

After this, I dealt from the shoe three twenty-ones in a row. They lost all their money.

"What did I tell you?" said the wise guy to his friend.

However, his friend, who had just complimented me and still lost all his money, took it in stride.

"Good thing that you took all my chips. You saved me the trouble of having to go to the casino cage and wait in line for their exchange to cash!" he responded with a grin.

After they left my table, I felt bad about their loss, but I could not influence the eight-deck shoe of cards for them, from which I pulled the cards that were dealt on the table. Even though they had just lost, they still left with smiles. They were responsible, and they knew when to stop.

Later on that day, two young men came to try their luck at my table, and after I requested their picture identification (in accordance with the policy of the casino and the requirements of gaming regulators), they were somewhat puzzled.

"Don't you see that we are already twenty-five years old?" one of them asked me.

"Looks can be deceiving, and we've got to be sure about your age because of the requirements of the Gaming Control Board," I responded.

They played slowly and asked many questions. One of them had never played the game before and asked his friend for advice.

"Shall I split my queens?" he inquired of his friend.

"Let's put it this way: if you have a good-size penis, you should not chop it in half," his friend wisely counseled him. Indeed, two queens are worth twenty and are considered a strong hand, whereas it is unpredictable if the hand is split what cards may then be dealt by the dealer.

They laughed and played until their last dollar.

At this time, there was a big game going on in the high limit pit. The high limit pit is where the so-called high rollers (large bettors) tend to place their large table-game bets. All the dealers were very interested in the action, especially one of my coworkers.

"We will make big tips today!" said my coworker.

Indeed, in these cases, when players are betting high, the dealers have a much better chance of receiving higher tips if the player wins. Table-game dealers get most of their salary from those patrons who have winning hands. Dealing a large winning hand to a high roller can often result in big gratuities being paid to the dealer at the table. These tips are then shared with all the dealers that worked that shift in the casino.

In this case, the gentleman who was playing in the high limit pit was middle-aged, relatively well off, and came from Texas. Unfortunately, he was not a professional gambler, who would know what to do and when to stop. At first, he played each of his hands for $500. Following a few lucky winning bets, he raised his individual bets up to $1,000 a hand. Then he raised his bets again to $3,000 a hand, while he was being dealt two twenty-ones or blackjacks.

He could leave the casino then as a winner. That was his moment, but he did not know it. As a novice, he was not aware of it. Sadly, he was determined to win more.

He did not know how to play the game, and he was already under the influence of alcohol, thanks to the convincing smile of the cocktail girl. Then he began to lose money. Then he lost some more. Yet he kept on playing, hoping to win it all back. There was an atmosphere of tense anticipation around this player. Some spectators held their breath. Perhaps an hour had passed, with more losing hands.

"Do you still have money to pay for your rent?" one of the women seated at his table asked.

"I do not have anything to worry about. In case I lose, I can always mortgage my farm," responded the high roller. That was a joke, but the women at the table did not like it.

As the table-game dealer later told me, the player did not follow good strategy. The high roller played his cards in a way that was not likely to yield a good outcome. For example, he had hit a hard seventeen. To hit means that he asked for more cards after the value of his cards already totaled seventeen, which is a reasonably good hand. He also split deuces and threes, against the dealer's face card, which is also bad strategy. All blackjack books on proper game strategy correctly advise table-game players to stand on hard seventeens and split only eights and aces.

While the high roller was playing, the pit supervisor changed the cards and also the dealer after a few hours. That was the time that player's luck began to run out. Yet he kept on playing and pressing his bets.

The following day, I heard that he lost $80,000 in total that night. Shortly thereafter, he jumped off the roof of the casino and died. His name was Jim. The casino's name is not important because it could happen in any casino. In fact, more than one casino has had similar situations in their past. All the casinos have their tragic moments and tragic stories.

In this instance, the casino's security guard called Jim's wife to notify her of the suicide. On the telephone, she told the security guard that her husband had already called earlier to tell her that he had lost $80,000, and she told him that "It is better you never come home anymore." She cried and said, "I did not really mean it; I was only angry for his loss."

With events like this associated with gambling, the question remains: is it worth it to put our life savings on any game, just for fun or for the thrill of the risk?

We have to keep in mind that all the beautiful casinos were built from those lost fortunes that were wagered on the casino's tables and machines.

Although people win from time to time, more often more of them lose and leave defeated. Mostly, the players are defeated by their own false sense of invincibility and greed—their belief that they will win big. It does not matter what the odds are. When players do not know the games, do not have luck on their side, or are too drunk to think right, they are not going to win.

Gambling can be great for entertainment and for excitement, but it is not wise to put our life savings or the farm on it. As in all things in life, our self-control and moderation are important factors in the world of games and gambling.

Gambling addiction is a mental disorder, but people do not look at it the way they should. Addicted people mostly stay addicted. They care more for their life-consuming addiction than anything else. They do not admit that they need treatment. Even treatment is not guaranteed to provide a cure, as some of the addictive behaviors are hardwired into our systems. As they sometimes say, "You cannot change the spots on the leopard." Yet a lot more should be done to avoid needless tragedies.

CHAPTER 2

HE WHO LOOKS FOR TROUBLE WILL FIND IT

The gambling capital of the world, Las Vegas, is an opulent oasis in the Mojave Desert. The famous forties gangster Bugsy Siegel would be happy to see how his idea of an upscale gambling destination ultimately became successful in this city, which now has a nonstop business cycle thanks to the success of resort gambling.

Las Vegas casinos are known for their versatile offerings and guest-friendly atmosphere. Such quality has drawn millions of people, in a relatively short amount of time, from all over the world.

In its character, Las Vegas has an international flair. It is also a place with libertarian attitudes, where not too many questions are asked and the success of casinos and other businesses is an important objective. Having created a success story in the desert, Las Vegas provides the opportunity for people from all over the world to win or lose money on any day of the week and at any time of the day. However, the glitter and excitement of Las Vegas sometimes come with unexpected surprises.

The majority of the guests like Las Vegas not just for its ubiquitous gambling opportunities, but also because they can have a lot of fun in the city in addition to spending time in the gambling halls. Deservedly, the city has approximately forty million visitors a year, and there is always something going on for even nongamblers to enjoy.

The overall visitation and interest in the city are positive. At the same time, it also attracts some unsavory characters, such as robbers, cheaters, confidence artists, pimps, prostitutes, and so on. Occasionally, the casinos' security systems fail to adequately deal with such issues. Such systems do not always quickly recognize criminal elements, elements that are clearly not optimal for the majority of the population, especially when they fall victim to a crime.

One of the regular problems in the city is prostitution. While it is technically illegal, it is a "service" that is widely available for those who wish to find it. Unfortunately, prostitution is often connected to other crimes, such as theft and drug use. To make their money, prostitutes and their pimps are undeterred by any prohibitions in the law or otherwise.

Prostitutes are often successful in building up their business empire on the heels of the large number of willing buyers generated by the casino businesses. They succeed because they know how the system works and how to use the system to their advantage.

In the casinos, cash money changes hands by the minute. Indeed, it is the nature of gambling that money itself is seen as something that can be easily acquired with very little real effort, albeit it is just as easily spent or lost. At the same time, the free drinks that are being provided by the house further help to grease the wheels of the industry and stimulate demand. This environment attracts lots of patrons who look for easy money and easy pleasures.

As such, it is not surprising that, in Las Vegas, we do not have to look for trouble; instead, trouble will occasionally find us.

People who drink a lot often will lose more than they can afford. Given their inebriation, they also lose control over their judgment and their behavior. By losing control, they are easy targets for criminals.

In this environment, patrons are also more likely to let out their frustrations with their lives or their luck, often cursing regularly. As one of my friends once noted, f-bombs are flying in the casinos, as pigeons are flying down from city rooftops.

Prostitutes like the casino environment; they look at it as their hunting ground. In this, they are often ignoring the laws of the city, the regulations of the house, and the general expectations of the public at large.

Of course, while the "working girls" are doing their business in a discrete manner, acting as "girlfriends" to patrons, nobody will bother them in the casinos. It is as if there is a secret mutual pact between prostitutes and casinos: do not bother us, and we will not bother you.

Naturally, most male patrons like the working girls. In fact, the presence of attractive women on the casino floor also attracts more business for the casinos. This becomes a symbiotic relationship, or a winning formula, for both industries. The girls make more money by having a wealth of inebriated male guests with loose cash around them, and the casinos make more money by having large groups of attractive and flirtatious women around the gaming space who attract more players to the games.

Many years ago, I was working in one of the casinos on the Las Vegas Strip when a group of Russian tourists arrived by bus for a three-day visit to Las Vegas on their way to San Francisco. Some members of the group went straight to the bar.

A few hours later, the casino manager asked me to come to the back office to help translate for one of the Russian tourists. Apparently, his money was stolen at the bar. Also present in the office were hotel security and a police investigator.

While I did learn Russian in school, I am not proficient by any means. However, listening to the Russian tourist's words, I could understand that two girls started to hug and kiss him at the bar, and one of them pulled out his money from his inside pocket. Shortly thereafter, the girls disappeared.

The security staff played back the surveillance tape associated with that particular casino bar. The Russian guest quickly recognized the girls in the video. Unfortunately, the police could not do anything about his stolen $1,400. The man cried because this money was all that he had brought with him for his US vacation.

"Sadly, they are hard to catch, as there are too many of them," explained the police investigator, "and they will not show up in the same place twice."

A few weeks after this incident, on a busy Saturday night, I was dealing cards on the blackjack table. It was a shoe game, which means that the cards, once shuffled, are dealt from an enclosed box on the table. At my table, patrons were able to bet between $300 and $500 per hand.

One of the players at my table, at the third base position, had already accumulated a nice collection of $500 chips in front of him, from a series of winning hands. However, he was somewhat drunk.

As we later understood, this was the opportunity for Sally, an attractive working girl, to show up with her two ugly duckling helpers at my table. The ugly ducklings were two apparent bodyguards for Sally, who stood farther behind them for security. After these events, some players remarked that the look of Sally's bodyguards destroyed not only their desire for sex but even their desire for life itself, as they looked very scary.

Having descended on my table with her team, Sally turned to the player with the big stack of five-hundred-dollar chips in front of him.

"What's up, asshole?" she greeted him. "I see that you are doing well."

"Excuse me, madam," I interjected, "but vulgar comments are not permitted in our casino. Please let our players enjoy the game."

"You just keep yourself busy with your shitty little low-paying job," she audaciously responded, "and mind your own damn business."

Then she continued with her vulgarities. In accordance with the casino's policies, I tried to call over the table-game supervisor, but he was too busy at another gaming table. Sally left, and I thought it would be okay—no more trouble.

Approximately a half hour later, Sally returned to my table with a couple of her prostitute friends. She placed a folded piece of paper in the high roller's hand; he still had a large stack of five-hundred-dollar chips in front of him. At the same time, she also pulled out a twenty dollar bill and handed it to me as a gratuity.

"Thank you," I told her, "but I did not deal cards for you at this table, so I cannot accept the gratuity."

"Don't be conceited with me because I have more money than you," she retorted. "Besides, I am going to nursing school!"

She then added a few more vulgarities. Given all that had transpired, my anxiety level further escalated. I tried to call the table-game supervisor again, but again he was unavailable. He was delivering money to another table game about ten feet away.

After the working girls left, the patron gave me Sally's piece of paper with her phone number for my protection, just in case Sally would later try to lodge a false complaint against me for improper customer service. Then he walked over to one side of the table game between us to hug me.

"You are nice," he said. "You protected me, and I love you for that."

"Thank you very much, sir," I responded, "but please stay on your side of the table, as patrons are not allowed inside the casino pit."

Finally, the table-game supervisor was able to come over to my table game. I could finally inform him about the whole situation.

Then Sally returned again. This time the supervisor called security right away. The casino's security guards escorted the prostitutes from the casino. Sally was mad.

"You destroyed my life!" she shouted to me on her way out.

However, she was just escorted out. As no crime had occurred, the casino did not call the police; they just wanted her to stop aggressively soliciting our patrons. The casino's security guards merely asked her not to return to our casino.

Following this incident, I thought to myself, while she may indeed aspire to be a nurse someday, given her aggressive personal style, I would not trust her even with my cat.

This was not my only experience with prostitution in Las Vegas. A few years later, I worked at another casino, where my friend and coworker was the central player in the next episode.

To protect his identity, let us call him Accidental John, or John for short. John was a nice and funny guy with a big heart. He often cooked delicious food at home and regularly brought some of his tasty food to work with him to share with his coworkers. He always complimented the ladies and told many funny jokes. Everybody liked him for his warm and personable style.

John, like me, was not a native speaker of the English language. This had, in our case, gotten him into trouble.

One day at work, the table-game supervisor called me to the pit telephone and told me that John was on the line and he wanted to speak to me. When I took the phone, John told me that he was in jail for a misunderstanding and I should bail him out. He assured me that he would pay me back later, once he was set free.

I began wondering what John could have done to be arrested. The following day, I went to the bail bond company with my cash savings, but it was not enough for the full amount of the bond. I also had to provide my car's title document to get sufficient money to bail John out from jail.

Once John was released from jail, he told me about his troubles.

"I went after work to the casino bar with our coworkers," he explained. "Then I had a couple of drinks. Then a woman approached me and told me that she would like my gold necklace."

John then took a deep breath.

"'*For how much?*' I asked her," John continued, "because I had another gold necklace at home. At that moment this lady said to me, 'Las Vegas Police Department' and placed the handcuffs on me. She told me that I was 'soliciting for prostitution.'"

John looked very sad.

"I could not believe that for offering to sell my gold necklace, I could be arrested," John said. "I guess my words of 'For how much?' were misunderstood. They told me that they thought I was asking her how much for her services."

If it was not for the fact that John already spent time in jail and my car's title documents were with the bail bond company, it would have been a funny story. I trusted John that he would pay me back. He told me that his money was in Budapest, Hungary, where both of us were from, and that he was going to bring the money back. In any event, he was ready to travel home to Budapest to visit his mother, because she was sick.

"I will come back; please do not worry," he told me.

Most of my coworkers predicted that John would not return from Budapest because of the criminal charges against him. However, he did return.

John went to the Las Vegas court with a professional translator at his side and explained to the court his meeting with the undercover agent at the bar. The prosecutor immediately dropped the charges. The bond was released. I got my car's title documents back from the bond company.

"You should teach John proper English, and do not let him visit any bars," said one of the security guards at the casino who was not so close to John.

"That would be like the blind leading the blind because my English is not that great either," I told him.

John then returned to work. He also took English as a Second Language classes with me. In the end, we had a happy ending. I was very pleased that he did not let me down and returned from Hungary to take care of everything the way he said he would.

My earliest experience with the prostitution industry was shortly following my arrival in this country. I knew much less about the ways of the West, and my English was also very limited at the time. I also did not know much about the context of want ads.

Considering my status then as a beginner, I also have to admit that my value on the job market was relatively low; only my determination to find a job was high. However, to improve my lot in life, I searched for a better job constantly.

One of my friends recommended that I look in the daily newspaper advertisements for jobs. Soon, I felt lucky enough to spot an ad for a "hostess job" with "competitive compensation," which also stated that a high level of English proficiency was not required. I figured that in dealing with the public, it would be easy to say such things as, "How are you today?" "This way please!" "Have a good time!" and the like. Naturally, I was very happy to spot this well-paid hostess position, although not all aspects of the job were summarized in the newspaper.

In preparation for the interview, I dressed in a conservative suit, wore high heels, and curled my hair. I wanted to look nice and pleasing. I tried my best to look good.

I went to the address provided. I arrived at the job site five minutes early.

My positive outlook, however, started to fade once I saw the place where I would be interviewed. Suddenly, I became suspicious. The place was old and run-down. I knocked on the door of the office that matched the address in the advertisement. A blond woman who opened the door greeted me with a strict expression on her face.

By the time her business partner showed up, I knew already that I was at the wrong place. The blond woman's business partner looked scary and intimidating. He might as well have been a cast member in the classic horror movie *The Addams Family*.

Soon, I saw a lot of white towels on a shelf and a lot of keys at the side of the front door.

"What will be my job?" I asked the blond woman politely.

In response, she pulled out the top drawer of an armoire that was at one end of the office and took out a mini black lingerie that barely covered the most intimate parts of a woman's physique.

"You are going to wear these, and you will have conversations with any man who comes here," she explained.

It was then that I was certain that my job search had ended in defeat. My eyes welled up with tears from this humiliating surprise and intimidation.

"Thank you, but my English is not good enough for this kind of conversation," I told her. "You could not advertise this job in my old country, because it would be prohibited as prostitution."

While my tears were running down my face, I quickly ran out from this place. I was scared that they would grab me and then drug me with some narcotics to put me to work.

Later my friends and family members at my birthday party tried to joke with me about the incident.

"It is nice to have a '*hostess*' like you with us, who cooks so well," they said.

Luckily, two weeks after this episode, I found a good job with the help of my friends as a real hostess in an upscale Italian restaurant. Later on, I would laugh about my misunderstanding of the job ad.

Prostitution has a long and contradictory history. It has existed since the beginning of recorded history. It is indeed the world's oldest profession. While the laws and regulations keep changing, the profession itself has not.

Patrons have always paid for sexual pleasure, especially those who had limited access to partners, fewer social skills, lower expectations, certain addictions, and the like. This profession would not exist if individuals were not willing to pay for the services of working girls. In some cases, of course, the workers would be men. In almost all cases, however, the patrons would be men.

Societies have different approaches to this issue. In most of the world, prostitution is legal, or those laws that may prohibit it are not enforced, except in the Middle East and the United States, where it is strictly prohibited and punished. In most Scandinavian countries, they only penalize those who solicit prostitutes, but not the sex workers themselves.

In my old country, Hungary, prostitution was illegal during the Communist era, and it was mostly prostitutes who were punished with jail. Following the fall of communism in 1989, they changed the law in Hungary. They now look at prostitution as a private entertainment business and the girls themselves as private contractors. They allow it in certain parts of the big cities so long as prostitutes are paying taxes and are carrying an unexpired state-issued health card. Pimping, however, is still strictly punishable as a crime, given its relationship to trafficking and the assumption of forced slave labor. Since it is a legal industry, sex workers can now go to the police for protection.

Such changes allowed the government to monitor health concerns and target sex trafficking, where the activity is not between consenting adults. In legalizing prostitution, their slogan was that "If you cannot change them, you might as well join them."

The debate over this ancient profession is endless, and most societies look at it as an unavoidable part of our social life. In my view, only legalization and strict regulation can help to ensure that its negative consequences are limited.

Because I am not a man, my personal experiences with prostitution were, of course, limited and different. Honestly, I found the entire industry personally irritating. Although prostitution may seem like an easy job and a well-paid job, in reality, it is just the opposite. Sadly, some girls have false illusions about it—illusions that are often cultivated by manipulative pimps.

The working girls are often pitiable. They are in business day and night and serve people who are often not at their best. Their patrons are often moody, perverse, rude, sadistic, and thankless.

At the same time, working girls usually have their own severe health and psychological problems as well. They have to be brave and determined to earn their money, especially if there is a pimp involved, who takes some of their money or, even worse, forces them into this work through abuse. Often, prostitutes have to face life-threatening danger and an enormous amount of stress because they go on "blind dates" every day, and with that goes a lot of uncertainty.

CHAPTER 3

THE SURPRISE

Our daily lives hold many surprises, some good and some bad. Sometimes such surprises are brought on by events outside our control, and sometimes they are provided by those people whom we thought we already knew. In this instance, Gary Markiz had organized for my coworkers and me one of the greatest and the best surprises.

Everybody had thought that Gary was all business. Everybody had thought that he was just another ordinary casino worker with a low-key approach and quiet personality—until the day of a special celebration.

I moved to the United States from Hungary in 1984. I knew very little about this part of the world, and even less about the local customs, culture, and general proclivities of the general population.

Some of my friends educated me about how different life can be here, along with the styles and personalities of those who live here. They told me that I had to remain open to new ideas and show a positive attitude toward my new experiences, but I should not trust anyone too much. "Las Vegas is not a town for putting a lot of faith in anyone or anything," I was often told.

I was also told that in Las Vegas, people are mainly interested in money and in business and that they have dollar signs in their hearts. I was advised that too much sentimentality can be perceived as a sign of weakness. Lastly, I was warned that great romance is reserved only for classic Hollywood movies.

Following such a sober introduction, I was not sure how my daily life would be, but believed that, in the end, everything would fall into place. I remained curious and optimistic.

A few years later, I was hired to work in a Las Vegas casino as a table-game dealer. I was inexperienced. I was told that I only spoke "Hunglish," by which they meant that my English did not follow the rules of English grammar or proper usage, which was coupled with my thick Hungarian accent. As the proverbial redheaded stepchild, I also had reddish-brown hair.

All of these things sometimes provided a reason for some patrons to give me a hard time. My accent and linguistic challenges created more troubles daily than I could handle.

At this time, I worked in a Las Vegas casino located in the old downtown portion of the city, where I first met Gary Markiz. Gary was a table-game supervisor. My prospects immediately improved under his supervision.

In appearance, Gary was an average person. He was not very tall or all that striking in his physique. However, he had a neat and pleasant look. He mostly wore gray suits and eyeglasses and carried an elegant black briefcase as a symbol of his professionalism.

However, in his mannerism and in his actions, Gary was not an ordinary person at all. During the four years that Gary and I worked together, he was always at the top of his game. He always acted as a consummate professional. In addition, he had good people skills, had a good sense of humor, and was always dependable.

As his staff, we could turn to him with any problem, because he would always find a way to help us. He was never unwilling. If he was asked for help, Gary would never make faces or bad comments. He was patient and attentive. He cared about those who worked for him. All his staff loved him a lot for such qualities.

The Golden Rule to "Do unto others as you would want others to do unto you" was well represented in Gary's actions and personality.

However, in the casinos, other rules are observed and thought to be the golden rules. First and foremost, casino management requires that dealers follow the general rule that "Dealers should keep their mouths shut and deal." Given this rule, to talk about casino matters or to express any dissent were grounds for immediate termination.

As such, a casino is run much like an authoritarian regime. As management often explained, "A casino is neither a court of justice nor His Majesty's ballroom; a casino is solely designed to be a money-making factory. No arguments and no complaints are welcome from our employees."

Another formulation of such a rule was that "The boss is always right, and in case he is not, the same rule still applies."

I often thought that fairness to employees and the appreciation of employees were not something to which casinos would ever aspire. Sadly, besides these guiding principles that we, as employees of the casinos, needed to daily observe, our patrons were also presenting us with a mixed bag of treatment. We had to endure about as many insults as there were compliments.

However, Gary was undeterred. He always kept to the true Golden Rule. He always had words of wisdom, even when dealing with those patrons who were the most troubled or acted in the ugliest manner. Gary was always ready to do good things. Everybody was happy to see him around.

He made our days as employees easier and better with jokes. He also came to rescue us from rude and unjust customers.

"Do not forget, you are the better person to be able to control your emotions and solve a difficult situation like this," he used to say to us following a difficult guest encounter. Hearing his soothing words, we would always feel better.

I remember that our casino was often packed to the rafters with patrons, some of whom were not necessarily the best-quality persons. We often had troublemakers who gambled a lot, drank a lot, and cursed a lot. When they lost all their money, they took out their anger on the dealers.

Then Gary would appear at our tables like a Grail Knight, with a big smile on his face.

"We love you, sir. Unfortunately, the system is not perfect. But what the heck, it is only money. Tomorrow will be another day with new opportunities. May I offer you a complimentary lunch or dinner?" he would often say.

Following Gary's presentation to an irate patron, things calmed down, and cooler heads prevailed.

On a regular workday, Gary came to the table where I was dealing cards and asked me if I could go with him and some coworkers to the Little White Wedding Chapel the following day.

"After work, we are going to have a small celebration, because two of our coworkers, Sheldon and Diane, are getting married. Following the ceremony, we will have a private party across the street from the chapel, at the Blue Bird Restaurant," he explained.

So the next day, I arrived at the Little White Chapel. Everybody was there and dressed up for the occasion. Many of the women present in the chapel wore long dresses and likely spent that morning at their hair salons. Sheldon and Diane were dressed up the most for this celebration, wearing beautiful royal blue garments, with white flowers pinned to their lapels.

The chapel itself was thoroughly ornamented with many flowers, including pink roses and white lilies. There were also stunning spotlights, judiciously placed throughout. The place looked warm and inviting.

Many in the wedding party were in a sentimental mood. They were telling jokes and sharing stories about their own weddings.

"It is easy to get married in Las Vegas, as we are famous for fast weddings. However, what may happen afterward will be another story," joked one of them.

Indeed, in Las Vegas, some wedding chapels have a drive-through window, so that the ceremony can be conducted in the car, with the newlyweds saying their wedding vows through the car windows.

"I have to stop smoking because Diane will put me out on the balcony," Sheldon then said.

Sheldon and Diane shared with us that they were both previously married and had divorced a long time ago.

"Our first marriages were only good, it seems, for practicing and learning what we want and need," explained Diane.

This reminded me of my own marriage, which ended after nine difficult years with a complicated divorce.

We were all in a good mood and ready to walk into the chapel when Gary's wife, Kelly, arrived. She wore a black sophisticated dress with a little white rose. She was slim and pretty, and her long blond hair added a glow to her presence.

In coming to the wedding, Gary told his wife, Kelly, as she told us later, that they would be the witnesses for Sheldon and Diane's wedding. Afterward, they would celebrate together with the coworkers their fifth-year wedding anniversary.

Once Gary and Kelly arrived, Sheldon and Diane started to walk toward the entrance of the chapel. At the entrance of the chapel, Gary Markiz went down on one knee, pulled out a beautiful ring, and asked Kelly to remarry him.

"You romantic fool, you should have prepared me for this, but yes, yes, a hundred times yes. I love you," Kelly said.

All of us were very much touched by this moment, as well as surprised by Gary's actions; he had always seemed to us a perfect businessman, but not a really romantic person.

Later, Kelly told us that five years earlier, they could not afford an expensive wedding, and as such, Gary wanted to make up for it now. However, Gary had kept his idea secret to the last second. He pretended that he was only a wedding organizer for Diane and Sheldon. He gave all of us a great surprise, not only with the wedding but also with his romantic side.

In the end, Gary and Kelly had a double wedding with Sheldon and Diane. It was very impressive. It was twice as nice—not only because it happened the second time in their lives, but also for the special surprise it represented.

We all long for true love and happiness, but during my lifetime, I have never had an occasion like the one Gary had created for his wife and for all of us. I liked Gary's surprise wedding a lot, and many years later, I still remember all of it as if it happened yesterday.

With his surprise, Gary will always be near to my heart for his kindness and for his thoughtfulness, because he made me believe in the goodness of human beings again. There are many heartwarming occasions and benevolent individuals in this world. These are the things that give us purpose to live and make us feel good about our lives.

In the end, the sober information that my friends gave me at the beginning about my future in Las Vegas was only generally true, because Gary Markiz proved that not everything is about business in this city and that love and respect are more important than money.

Gary Markiz, my boss, was a great businessman and a true romantic at the same time. He was a "Mister Valentine" in his heart and a genuinely nice person in his daily life and in all his business affairs.

CHAPTER 4

THIS IS NOT MY CUP OF TEA!

In many West Coast cities, including Las Vegas, daily life becomes very limited and difficult without having a well-running car. In Las Vegas, the public transportation lines only became more developed during the last fifteen years.

The Las Vegas climate is also a challenge. Even if it is more affordable to travel by bus in those locations where they are conveniently available, not everybody is fit for this type of travel in the sweltering heat and burning sun of the Las Vegas summer months. Also, while buses are required to run in accordance with a schedule, they cannot always keep to it in this city and often provide unpredictable service.

While I worked very hard for many years to save up for a good car, I never had a car without headaches. This is true even though my last two cars were purchased brand-new.

When we first moved to Las Vegas, my son and I looked for jobs near to our apartment so that we could survive without cars. After we got our driver's licenses, we started to buy older used cars. But with older used cars came endless headaches. Even though we bought cars from "reputable" dealerships, each used car we bought turned out to be worse than the others.

Following one purchase, a day after we took the car home, the car's engine blew up in the middle of the road. As we later learned, this had happened because the distribution gear and the timing chain were both cracked. At the time of the purchase, the car dealer seemingly forgot to tell us about it.

"Here is your chariot, madam! This car is in great condition, and we also put extra gasoline in it for you," said the salesperson the day before as he handed me the car keys. "By the way, our mechanic just examined the car, and everything is in tip-top shape," he added.

But it was not to be. This car had one problem after another. The financial costs of repairs kept adding up. Of course, first the engine blew up. Just to rebuild the engine cost $1,200, not to mention all the other repairs that also had to be made.

"Mom, from now on, we will only buy new cars; we are not going to buy somebody else's headache," my son told me after the fifth time we were taking the "chariot" for additional repairs.

A year later, I purchased an attractive brand-new white Mazda Protégé. It had a moonroof and all creature comforts. Then, three years later, after I had just finished paying for the car in thirty-six monthly installments, a maroon-colored minibus plowed into my car at an intersection.

The accident took place at the entrance of the I-15 freeway that runs through Las Vegas. The two Hispanics in the vehicle did not have the time to wait until the light turned green and the cars ahead of me could drive away. Instead, they just rammed my car on its side and rear. They made a complete pile of junk out of my just-paid-for car.

Their engine was still running when the police arrived. However, they also did not wait for the police to arrive. Instead, they abandoned their car in the middle of the road and ran away and disappeared without a trace. As the investigation later revealed, they gave a phony address for the vehicle's registration and also had an expired insurance policy. I stood there with my newly paid-off Mazda that had been totaled. I cried.

"I am not lucky. I just paid off my car, and now look at it," I said to the policeman at the scene.

"I look at you, and I think that you are very lucky that you survived this accident without more serious injuries," said the policeman with a friendly smile.

Following the accident, my neck and my shoulder were in a lot of pain. I was in physical therapy for a few months, but nothing else happened. The policeman was right. I was really lucky that I could walk away from the accident in one piece on my own two feet. My car was replaceable, but not my life was not.

Unfortunately, the insurance company paid only half the value of my totaled Mazda, but at least I got some money for it. In the end, this new car cost me more than $20,000, and I only got $11,000 for it from the insurance reimbursement following the accident.

"Now you should buy a car that will also be more fun for you. Why don't you buy a nice Viking GTA Racer?" my son suggested to console me.

The next day we went to the Viking dealership. I did end up buying a Viking GTA Racer because I liked the stylish look of the car, its comfortable seats, and its wide stance on the road.

"This was a great idea! I'll enjoy driving this car," I kept telling my son.

I would only drive my Viking in the city—mostly to and from work and to do some shopping or errands. I had very low mileage on it.

My new Viking was only two years old when I started to get marketing telephone calls from the Viking dealership. They said that the new federal stimulus package gave me an opportunity to upgrade my car for the newest model with a moonroof for just a small incremental increase in price and with a lifetime warranty. Their offer was very tempting, especially with the lifetime warranty. I even called my son on the telephone to tell him about this great offer.

"Mom, please wait for me; we will go together on the weekend," he said.

"I am a big girl, and I do not want to waste your free time with my car deals," I told him.

"Please be careful; you know these car dealers already," he said.

"I'll be okay," I told him, "and if the new car would cost too much, I will not buy it. Besides, the Viking is very reputable."

So I went to the Viking dealership. I got a charming Italian American salesperson, who showed me the newer cars. They were nice and shiny. He also talked to me about the benefits of their lifetime warranty program. I ended up buying a brand-new beige GTA Racer with moonroof and shiny wheels. It was the latest model. Then the salesman left me to discuss the final particulars with his manager.

"You are a nice lady. Now you will have a nice brand-new car too, with a lifetime warranty. You only have to pay three hundred and eighty dollars for a year, and then the car is yours in exchange for your used car," the salesman told me upon his return.

My existing car was in perfect shape and had low miles.

"Okay, I'll do it. It seems like a good deal," I told him.

"It is possible only because of the stimulus package that the company got from the federal government," he told me.

Then the dealership began preparing the large volumes of paperwork on the exchange of the two vehicles—my relatively new GTA Racer and the brand-new and upgraded version of the same. The staff at the dealership also emptied out the contents of my car before I could even sign the contract. Unfortunately, I left my reading glasses in the other car. They told me I should not worry because they were going to mark the spots where I had to put my signature on the contract.

I had a complimentary cup of coffee while I waited for the paperwork. Finally, they called me into the office to sign it.

"So this is a one-year deal?" I asked the very polite Italian American salesperson again.

"Yes. Do not worry; I already marked the places on the contract where you have to sign it," he explained.

I was very grateful to him for his help and assistance and went home with the new car.

That same evening, my son came to visit me at my home and asked me about the contract. I told him how happy I felt about the purchase.

"For the first time in my life, I got a great deal on a brand-new car with a lifetime warranty," I told him.

My son read the contract, and his face turned increasingly serious.

"Mom, this is not a one-year financing agreement; this is a five-year financing agreement," he told me with shock on his face.

"That is impossible. The salesperson was very nice, and he told me specifically that it was a one-year deal," I said.

"It does not matter what he told you. Did you read the contract?" my son asked.

"I did not because my glasses were in my old car and they had already put my stuff in the new car. When I told them I needed my reading glasses, they said no worries; they would mark the spots where I needed to sign, which I did on the pages and pages of paperwork they gave me. They just marked the places where I had to sign it," I told my son as my tears started to fall.

We went back to the dealership immediately and talked to the salesperson who sold me the car.

"As far as I know, she signed a one-year deal," he explained to my son.

My son showed him the paperwork and asked him to call the manager. The manager was not surprised at all.

"She signed it," said the manager. "This is already a done deal. I cannot and I will not do anything for you."

My son gave his business card to the manager.

"You are going to hear from us soon," my son told the manager as we were leaving.

While I was still crying and my son was also saddened and upset by the unfair conduct of the dealership, the dealership's entire sales team was visibly laughing at us. We could see this as we looked back through the big glass windows of the dealership.

The next day, my son, who is an attorney, sent a three-page demand letter to the car dealership's owner. In the letter, he explained the dealership's unfair and improper conduct and threatened to sue the dealership for elder abuse. I was in my sixties at the time.

Upon receipt of my son's letter, the general manager of the Viking dealership called my son right away.

"Tell your mom," said the general manager, "that she can choose any car on our lot with a great discount, or if she wants, she can have her old car back, and we will give back her deposit."

Hearing the news of this, I was happy, and I decided that I would just take back my old car—which was still almost new and had very low miles on it.

I said thank you to my son.

"Who needs a car with a moonroof," I asked him, "if it costs that many headaches? My face burns easily and turns red from the sunlight in Las Vegas's sun anyway. Sadly, some of the salespeople at the car dealership did not have any redness or sensitivity on their faces when they tried to cheat me."

I went back with my son to the dealership to exchange the cars. I was very proud of him. This time the manager acted like a beaten dog. He was not laughing anymore. If anything, he was overly polite. They washed my old car before returning it. They even filled it up with gasoline, and all the while, the general manager apologized once a minute.

"What a difference a letter can make in twenty-four hours. It is unbelievable," I told my son as we were leaving.

I do not think that I will ever go to any car dealerships alone again in the future. Prior to this experience, the last time I felt I was defrauded was when one of the department store assistants charged me for her personal shopping on my department store charge account. Luckily, I recognized the fraud in time; otherwise, it would have meant more money lost.

Months after my ill-fated car-buying episode, I shared my GTA Racer story with one of my coworkers at the casino. She was not surprised at all.

"I would rather jab a sharp stick in my eye than set my foot in any car dealerships," she said and explained that "I let my husband deal with these sharks. It is not my cup of tea!"

"It cost me a day filled with worries and a sleepless night, but I got to the same conclusion," I told her.

Following the aforementioned exchange of the GTA Racers, had the salesperson not confirmed to my son that "This is a one-year deal," which is what the salesperson had always told me, my son would have thought that I'd lost my mind. I would not believe in a million years that a reputable and legitimate car dealership might still try to rip people off, as they did me, with their bald-faced lies.

Before my son's demand letter, the dealership ridiculed us that we wanted to set aside this deal. I felt ashamed of myself that I did not read over the many pages of their contract and trusted them blindly that it said what they had promised. My lack of observance of the basic rule that we have to read anything before we sign it caused sleepless nights and disappointment.

One of the most important ingredients of any human relationship is trust. Yet we cannot waste it on people who are unworthy of it.

A few weeks after my ill-fated exchange of the GTA Racers, this Las Vegas Viking dealership declared bankruptcy. It was not because of my specific car deal, but for other reasons. However, it did not surprise us at all, given the way that they had first misled me and then ridiculed me.

I did not pity them at all; rather, I pitied the customers who needed to deal with these kinds of tactics. To communicate with this dealership was definitely not my cup of tea either.

Regardless of how important transportation cars can be, car dealerships should be more truthful in general and less calculating with their customers' money in particular. In fact, car buyers often have difficult financial circumstances and desperately need a car. An honest deal should be important also for car dealerships if they want to stay in business over the long term.

CHAPTER 5

THE SNAKE

Although Las Vegas is in the Mojave Desert, it is surrounded by beautiful mountains and lots of outdoor recreational activities, including Lake Mead, the Colorado River, Mount Charleston, and the Red Rock Canyon National Conservation Area (". My favorite outdoor activity in Las Vegas is to spend time at Spring Mountain Ranch State Park's main ranch house, which houses the Eva Krupp Museum; the state park is completely within Red Rock Canyon NCA.

Following my arrival to Las Vegas, my son and I would often go see the wild donkeys or burros and the other desert animals that make their homes in Red Rock Canyon. As you would drive down the main road in Red Rock Canyon, you could see the donkeys walking down peacefully by the side of the road. It seemed that they enjoyed our visit, as much as we enjoyed visiting them. They were very friendly.

"Mom, are we going to see our relatives today?" my son would sometimes ask me in jest.

"Yes, *your relatives.* I think they already miss you," I would answer teasingly.

We would then both laugh about this on our drive out to Red Rock Canyon. We liked these excursions because of the beauty of nature, which helped to reduce our stress levels and make us feel liberated from the Las Vegas casino environment, where both of us worked for many years.

Nature is God's gift to mankind. Our spirits were always lifted by seeing the beauty of the mountains and the variety of living things that nature had brought forth. We enjoyed seeing the endless rows of huge cacti and Joshua trees along the sides of the road.

Usually on the way home from Red Rock Canyon, we would go eat at a Chinese restaurant our favorite dish, chicken chow fun. It is a dish made with wide rice noodles. While I liked to cook occasionally, it was nice to get a rest from household chores following the excursion. It was also fun to enjoy the ethnic food of a different culture—to experience its unique flavors and cooking styles.

In my spare time, I would also spend a lot of time watching the Animal Channel on television, because their programming often included interesting nature documentaries. In particular, I was always amazed by their snake documentaries. In one episode, they showed that certain individuals shared a tiny apartment with a bunch of poisonous snakes. In this instance, they all ended up dead, because the emergency responders did not arrive in time with the necessary antivenom after their snakes escaped and bit the occupants of the apartment.

As I learned from watching the Animal Channel, there are five states in the United States where they do not even require an exotic animal permit in order for someone to keep such dangerous animals as pets. Even in most of those states where a permit is required, a person can fairly easily keep a dangerous animal as a pet provided that he or she is at least sixteen years of age, has the right type of cage for these animals, and pays approximately thirty dollars for the associated permit. Beyond such skeletal requirements, there is no other hurdle that any would-be owner of a dangerous animal has to overcome. For example, the applicant's prior track record of correctly keeping such dangerous pets does not need to be demonstrated to authorities.

In another Animal Channel television show, they showed that in the Florida Everglades, very dangerous snakes, such as Burmese pythons, are overproducing. Such snakes deposit hundreds of eggs at a time. These snakes can trace their ancestry to snakes that have escaped from private owners or were released by private owners.

In fact, the most dangerous snakes, including the Burmese python and cobras, made their way into this country as a result of private purchases. Sometimes they were smuggled in. Sadly, once private owners were unable to properly care for or handle their snake collections, they ended up releasing them in the Everglades and in other wild places around the country. To first import such highly poisonous or dangerous snakes and then to release them into our local environment is highly irresponsible.

Through their careless actions, such snake collectors endangered other people's lives, as well as upset the existing balance of nature. In many cases, these exotic snakes are too big and too aggressive. When they sense human beings or animals with their heat detectors and chemical sensors, they sometimes go on the attack with deadly force, instead of hiding like indigenous snakes tend to do.

Pythons have teeth that act as hooks, with almost no one being able to escape their grasp. They can be as long as twenty-three feet. They are the biggest snakes in the world. They have already killed people in Florida. A cobra killed someone in Texas. A cobra's poisonous neurotoxin can cause respiratory or heart failure, with death occurring in one hour.

These nonnative snakes are also damaging to the native wildlife, especially the bird population. Small animals also become their victims. Pythons kill by constricting their victims, while they also plunge their sharp teeth into their victims. Luckily, pythons have poor eyesight; otherwise they would have more victims.

On a Sunday afternoon, my son and I, along with some of my friends, decided to drive out to Red Rock Canyon for our usual tour. It was a hot summer day; even the desert plants looked desiccated. The donkeys did not show up as usual. Most likely, they were hiding in the shade.

We passed by the giant red rocks and finally arrived at our destination, near the main ranch house at the Spring Mountain Ranch. The State Park Service provides picnic areas, with tables, in close proximity to the main ranch house, in the protective shade of big pine trees. These big pine trees tend to be surrounded by squirrels.

We sat down and took out our cold drinks and snacks from our cooling bag. One of my friends decided to give his peanut snack to the squirrels. Seeing the peanuts, the squirrels came closer to us to eat them. They seemed to be happy and playful.

We watched children playing ball on the grass in front of the main ranch house. The grass was lush and green because of the sprinkler system. Approximately fifteen children played ball with their teacher on the grass.

We walked toward the main ranch house to see the Eva Krupp museum inside, with all its old furniture and clothing. Not long after I stepped inside the museum and entered one of its smaller rooms, I heard the museum security guard shout: "Freeze!"

I quickly turned around. There was a huge diamondback rattlesnake under the table within striking distance from my leg. I naturally felt horrified, although the snake appeared somewhat relaxed. It was coiled up in the shape of a garden hose under the table to my left.

I could not determine its exact length or where exactly its head was. However, it appeared to have a total length of approximately seven feet, more or less; I could not see all its dimensions from the top of the table.

Regardless of its size, the snake represented real danger. I remember thinking to myself that it would have been better to wear long pants and sports shoes on this particular day. My friends and my son did not enter the room with the snake, but from a distance I could see that they looked worried to see me motionless and in danger. I thought to myself that I'd better start reciting the Lord's Prayer, as death might be imminent.

Fortunately, just at that moment, the museum's security guard thrust a long stick at the snake next to me with a hook on one end and quickly captured the snake, without even stepping any closer.

Luckily, rattlesnakes and other native snakes to Las Vegas avoid human contact at all cost and will bite only if they feel cornered or if they are captured. Albeit the snake did get captured by the guard, it did not apprehend what was happening until it was already safely captured. Still, I felt scared, because it could have just as easily happened that the snake got spooked and bit me.

I was near enough to the snake's hiding place to be bitten—within striking distance. Indeed, a snake can quickly lunge at its perceived attacker, striking to a distance of about a third of its body length.

While I understood that, even if I had been bitten by the snake, antivenom would likely be quickly available, it was no comfort. With a bite, there would still be a lot of pain, not to mention the snake injecting its hemotoxin into my bloodstream, thereby causing further tissue damage and destruction to my red blood cells. I thought to myself, *a snakebite is the last thing I need—my red blood cell count is already low from all the daily hard work at the casino.*

Luckily, the snake was on its way out. All of us that witnessed the incident were curious what would happen with the snake. We followed the museum's security guard from a distance of about fifteen feet. We saw that he dropped the big snake behind the fence surrounding the property, approximately forty or fifty feet from the small children who were still playing ball on the grass in front of the main house.

"This is way too close to people," I said to my son. "I am shocked. I do not think that the snake will ask for permission to return to our area, especially since there are many squirrels here that he can feed on. And the little kids' ball could also end up near where the snake was just released, resulting in a horrible bite."

"I hope that the snake is as scared as we are," my son comforted me, "and, hopefully, it will go hide, or at least, will give a fair warning with its tail."

"It is nice to be surrounded by nature, but also sometimes seems scary," our friends commented. "We are lucky that nothing happened today. One of our friends had an encounter with a mountain lion in California and was lucky to survive. Luckily, the puma was too busy eating its prey, and far enough away that he could quickly get back inside his nearby car."

"In my old country, if something like this would happen, they would take the snake in a cage to a zoo, or if there was no nearby zoo, only release the snake in a most remote area, where there were no people nearby," I commented.

I thought that maybe the park service had too many snakes at Red Rock Canyon to try to do the same. Perhaps they believed that snakes would just go and hide and human beings had an obligation to watch out for their own safety.

"I've had enough fun for one day," I said. "I surely will not visit the Spring Mountain Ranch too often, as I am not a big fan of snakes. I do not even like them in the form of handbags or jackets. They may look nice from a distance as part of nature, but they are way too dangerous for me to admire up close. I could not handle being close to them, even with the help of exposure therapy."

To be honest, I was also concerned by the security guard's actions in releasing the dangerous snake so close, just on the other side of the fence. I thought to myself I should probably stop going to the Mojave Desert, where they live, especially since I do not even have any kind of training to handle them.

"You are a lucky survivor," teased one of our friends.

We then considered going to Mount Charleston. However, this was at the same time that wildfires had just damaged the trees on Mount Charleston. As such, we could no longer visit there following this failed visit at Red Rock Canyon, because seeing the burned out and destroyed trees would fill us with sadness. Besides, the encounter with the snake was enough drama for one day.

So, following our adventure at Red Rock Canyon that had been cut short, we returned to the city and went to celebrate one of our friends' birthday at our favorite Italian restaurant.

"I enjoy getting presents from my boyfriend," my girlfriend said at dinner. "He always has such great surprises. The last time he gave me a little dog in a beautiful box. It is great to have good friends, like my boyfriend, like you guys, and share such experiences."

"I feel the same way, except for surprises that come to me," I told her. "Surprises, good or bad, to me can also be at times stressful, and I have had too many such surprises in the past."

Of course, part of this was my encounter with the snake. Our friends and I wanted to also celebrate the happiness and relief that I felt that I avoided being bitten by the snake. Indeed, it made me feel very good to be so lucky.

Las Vegas and its natural surroundings have an amazing beauty. I never liked reptiles, although they are part of nature. In this instance, I was lucky to survive our visit at Red Rock Canyon, where apparently so many snakes live. This completely unexpected close encounter with a diamondback rattlesnake raised my stress level significantly at the time. Yet afterward, it made me happy that I was able to survive a situation that could have quickly turned bad. I know that nothing can be taken for granted in our lives.

There are always unexpected surprises in our lives, with which we have to cope, and we are lucky when we do so. If I could chose them, I would, of course, only I would want to have good surprises only and no more close encounters with snakes.

The diamondback rattlesnake is a beautiful creature, but it is also a feared predator, as it can be deadly and aggressive. When it rattles its tail, it provides its last warning that you are intruding and you should back up. In my case, I did not get such a warning, because the museum's security guard was able to quickly grab the snake with his stick. I was very lucky indeed.

Nature that surrounds us is God's beautiful creation, but we should not bother animals in their natural habitats and territory. Before we visit nature, we should try to learn its ways. Of course, I do not mind any wild predatory animal, so long as it does not approach me, as I am scared of them. I wonder how some people can live under one roof with poisonous reptiles and other dangerous animals. Following my encounter with the snake, all I can say is that I am happy to still be alive.

"Mom, nature is still beautiful," my son pointed out, "so please, forget about the snakes. The next time, we'll visit only the donkeys!"

"Yes, you Silly Billy," I responded, "but I will only visit the donkeys if they are coming to see us without a snake's escort. For sure, I should take snake-charming classes before our next adventure."

Some people like this kind of excitement. They like to flirt with danger. Some enjoy the thrill of the risk with a dangerous snake. But while the thrill of the risk may be tempting, such dangerous adventures do not always have happy endings.

We always have to make choices in life. In certain situations, we have to place our own safety above the short-lived thrill, fun, or excitement. Our good health and our lives are irreplaceable.

CHAPTER 6

WHY ARE THEY SHOOTING?

If all of humankind would appreciate human life on this planet, it would be a beautiful place to live. We could all live in peace and comfort. Sadly, a small number of crazy individuals choose to destroy their environments and the lives of others.

Amazingly, such individuals have no appreciation for anything. They do not care about the value of other people's lives. They are either mentally ill or so corrupted by evil thoughts that they can only take pleasure in death and destruction. Unfortunately, incidents of vandalism and terrorism are repeated all around our world.

When I look back at my own life, all I can say is that I have been very fortunate. I had many fulfilling experiences, where I met many nice people, who helped me and loved me. Luckily, there are a lot more good people in this world than bad.

However, over the years, I also unfortunately had to witness some disturbing and shocking events, which were difficult to cope with at the time. Some of these events involved shootings, while other events involved unexpected human interactions.

For a normal person, it is difficult to understand what a crazy person who chooses to shoot and kill dozens had hoped to gain besides putting his contempt for society on display.

The constitutional right to bear arms does not, of course, mean that one can shoot and kill people randomly or terrorize entire neighborhoods. However, it also does not mean that one should amass an arsenal of dozens of high-powered weapons. For self-defense, when needed, a couple of guns should suffice. We have only two hands after all.

Is there a war going on? I wonder to myself whenever I see a news story involving mass shootings. *No, of course not.*

Yet some are behaving as if there were a war—or worse. Some deranged individuals shoot and kill people just for the fun of it.

One time when I was listening to the news, I was astonished to hear about two shooters' horrific acts of violence. I telephoned my son right away and told him what was being reported on the news and that the active shooters were on the move.

"Please do not worry," my son told me. "The police will catch the shooters."

"Yes," I said, "but the real question is when. How many more victims will have to die in the meantime?"

"Hopefully no one else," my son replied. "Mom, you watch too many of these things on the news. We should worry only about things that we can change. That in itself is enough to deal with. Please do not stress yourself out because of these murderous criminals. Sadly, there have always been and there will always be people like them."

I just cannot understand what these individuals gain by shooting and killing innocent people they do not even know. Their action is pure insanity. No one will have a better future or be better appreciated as a result of this kind of shameful act.

Earlier in human history, some people killed others over religious and cultural differences, as well as for women, for resources, and for territory. In response, people have also killed others in self-defense. In modern societies, we still have killing in the name of all the above, as well as for fun or for purely evil purposes. Sadly, some of these evil acts seem to go on in ever greater numbers now.

Part of the problem is that technology enabled those with sick and evil intentions to create greater carnage. Guns and bombs can more quickly do more damage than a knife. Additionally, a modern and free society is more exposed to such threats than an intrusive and controlling dictatorship, which constantly spies on and is committed to controlling its citizens.

We will not know in each case as to why someone might engage in mass shootings because different people may be motivated by different irrational reasons. After their horrific acts, they try to disappear and not be apprehended. In most cases, they are shot dead before they can be interrogated.

"There are always bad eggs in every basket," my friend once told me. "These mass shooters and killers do not deserve to live."

Sadly, these unanticipated mass shootings are now in schools, malls, churches, movie theaters, restaurants, and other public places—everywhere where one would in the past not have anticipated them.

Anyone who commits this kind of criminal act is either mentally ill or so evil that he or she does not care about the consequences. These types of people also do not care about their own lives. From news reports, it is apparent that such perpetrators usually have mental issues. They do not have the feeling of belonging. They often have narcissistic motivations—to do something outrageous through which the world will remember them.

Many have identified the lack of adequate gun control regulations and the lack of early identification and proper treatment for the mentally ill as two of the contributing causes for such violence. Indeed, we should have stronger gun control laws with fewer loopholes and a more thorough system of background checks. We should also improve the process for the early identification and proper treatment of the mentally ill.

Yet there are also other significant reasons for this type of dissociative behavior, some of which are related to family life. In particular, while the mentally ill are taught normalcy by professionals, they are frequently still unable to function normally without help and supervision at home. They need the constant companionship of a responsible caretaker to help them, to make sure that they take their medication on time and go to treatment regularly. Sadly, they do not always have such oversight.

Our immediate environment is one of the greatest determinative factors for our lives. Yet some parents do not have the time or inclination to teach their children about respecting others and about the value of human life. In some cases, the parents themselves do not appreciate the rule of civilization for thousands of years that you should treat people the way you yourself want to be treated. "Do to others what you want them to do to you," or the Golden Rule, should be taught repeatedly.

Each person begins his or her early life as a child as part of a learning process by learning behaviors and skills. In this process, motivations, belief systems, and emotional attachments play a key role. The parents, especially mothers, are firstly responsible for the proper early development of their children. Mothers are the ones who teach key adaptation skills to their kids. They show their offspring how to behave and how to respect and love others. Without these skills, their children will suffer, but society will also suffer.

"Respect yourself, and others will respect you" is another important maxim to learn. Indeed, when we learn to respect ourselves truly, we will not do anything that will embarrass us and put us to shame. This also ensures us that we will do good to ourselves and to others. We have to carry ourselves with respect so that others will respect us.

Our educational system is not as involved as it should be in teaching ethical behavior. For example, they should teach subjects such as ethics in high schools. They should also require responsible behavior from the students all the time and give them less freedom to do bad things. They should coach students to care for one another and for their environment.

At home, parents should not let their children watch crime reports, horror movies, and thrillers. Instead, they should talk with their kids more often, explain right from wrong in all contexts, and make sure that their children are engaged in healthy activities.

"What do you expect from this kind of people?" a friend of mine once commented. "Most likely their parents did not have a normal education or upbringing. It is likely that many of them were born out of wedlock."

Criminals and the mentally ill should not have guns, knives, or even sharp sticks. Yet one way or another, they are able to get these weapons most of the time. The person who illegally supplies them with deadly weapons should be held just as responsible as the ultimate perpetrator for their acts. Yet in some cases, they also fall as victims.

God gave us our lives for a reason—to help and to love one another. Our lives should not be wasted on evil and barbaric acts.

My personal involvement in a shooting came about very unexpectedly. In a way, I am lucky that I am still alive today.

I never had a gun. I did not even want to own one. First of all, I could not kill anyone with a gun, even it involved self-defense. Because I also lack the training to use a gun, it would not help me even if I had one. To me, a gun just seems useless.

I moved to the United States three decades ago at the time of the San Ysidro McDonald's massacre. The perpetrator shot and killed twenty-one people and injured nineteen others, including several children, before being fatally shot by a SWAT team sniper. For a long time, this shooting remained the deadliest mass shooting committed in the United States.

When I heard about this tragic event, I was really shocked. When the news report first came on my television set, I first thought that there was a revolution here. Then I was told that, unfortunately, something like this could happen at any time.

In Hungary, we did not have this kind of mass shootings at the time, albeit there may have been some lone wolves ready to do something crazy. In my old country, the biggest cause of heartbreak was our government and our political system.

In Hungary at the time, only the members of the military, the police, and professionals could own guns. We knew who our enemy was. Some people quietly disappeared without a trace under the Communist system. In secret, they were either killed or deported, with some being shipped as far as Siberia.

We also had plenty of shootings and violence during World War I, World War II, and the Hungarian Revolution of 1956 against Soviet and Communist rule. These were, of course, very different times. They involved all-out war and social conflict.

One day in Las Vegas, I had to go to the bank. I had already worked for a few years in the casino industry at the time. When I got to the bank, the members of the police department stopped me at the bank's entrance.

"Go home and be happy that you did not arrive ten minutes ago," one policeman told me. "A gang of robbers just ordered everybody down on the floor."

A couple of days later, I read in the newspaper that a man, out of revenge, drove an armored vehicle or tank inside his town's social security building. I feel that this kind of vehicle should only be available to the military, not to the general public.

America, of course, is the land of the free and the home of the brave. Yet insane individuals, by being able to purchase such highly dangerous war machines, violate all our freedoms. I am for responsible citizens being able to buy some guns, but this type of an arms race in the private sector goes way too far. It seems to me that when it comes to deadly weapons, some have negligently misinterpreted the meaning of "freedom." Our freedom to buy guns should only go as far as we can safely handle them.

"People should know where one person's freedom ends and where another person's freedom begins," as one of my friends once told me.

In addition to the bank incident, I also have been in other dangerous situations. As I was told, they were "only incidents."

One day when I went to work, at the entrance of my casino, our casino's security officers told me that I had to stop and could not go in. Because of a bomb threat made by a man named Arash Mohammed, hotel security had temporarily closed the facility. Apparently Mr. Mohammed got in some kind of argument with the front desk clerk and left a duffel bag at their counter. He told the front desk clerk that there was a bomb in the bag. Apparently he wanted revenge. In the end, however, it was just a fake threat.

In spite of strict security procedures, incidents involving violence or threats of violence occur with some regularity at casinos.

In one case, an upset patron started shooting at the New York New York Hotel and Casino, which is one of the major casinos on the Las Vegas Strip. The shots were fired in close proximity to the card tables. Apparently the patron was upset because he had just broken up with his girlfriend. Other patrons on the property, fearing for their lives, fled across the street for their safety to the casino that I was working at.

Another time, some individuals held up the Bellagio Hotel and Casino's main casino cage at gunpoint. Later I heard that this had happened more than once.

I also heard that someone set fire at the Sahara Hotel and Casino. Someone else then set fire at the Monte Carlo Hotel and Casino.

Do these people feel that their freedoms are unlimited? I thought to myself. Some of my acquaintances tried to convince me that these were just single and unusual incidents. Yet taken together, there were sadly just too many of them.

While I understand that Las Vegas may still be the Wild West in some ways, many such horrific acts are being repeated not just in this city but all over this country. Sometimes it even appears that there is some kind of antisocietal revolution going on. Certainly some criminals will shoot and kill innocent people even in the heart of our communities, including in our schools and churches.

I just do not understand why we have to have so many shootings, violence, or even intentionally set wildfires all across this land. All of us should be happy to live here in the land of opportunities. There are so many nice people and good things in this country. Indeed, this is one of the best countries in the world. We should all be happy to enjoy it and maintain it as such.

Perhaps if someone is caught for the commission of a violent crime, such a person should not be allowed to post bail and be released.

When a perpetrator kills solely for fun, it is the most cynical and pain-inducing act. It does not make any sense whatsoever. I often wonder whether these people did not have a mother or other strong positive influence in their lives that would teach them to respect human life.

In any event, I have always had my fingers crossed that this type of violent fate or misadventure would not befall me. I often tell my relatives, "No matter how I wish to avoid these things, I just cannot stay indoors at all times. I have a life to live."

At one time, I was just about to leave my apartment when I saw that the police had cordoned off my entire apartment complex. I asked one of the policemen nearby what was going on. The policeman told me that during the middle of the day, three teenagers were robbing people at gunpoint in our neighborhood. Apparently they had snuck up on their victims while the victims were busy taking their groceries out of their cars.

Only God knows why these *teenagers* had guns in the first place. Their parents probably did not know about it.

I felt that I had had enough of this nonsense. *Why am I always in the wrong place?* But I was not in the wrong place; I was at home. Sadly, such things now happen too regularly. Too often, such an event does not get the level of publicity that it deserves. Understandably, those who are worried that these events could harm the reputation of Las Vegas tend to keep their reporting to a minimum.

In 1997, the Evander Holyfield vs. Mike Tyson II fight, later referred to as The Bite Fight, was a big attraction in Las Vegas. It achieved notoriety as one of the most bizarre fights in boxing history after Tyson bit off part of Holyfield's ear in the third round. Tyson was disqualified from the match and lost his boxing license, though it was later reinstated.

Following the fight, there was a huge crowd of upset Los Angeles residents roaming the casinos, including ours. Many of them had made losing bets on the fight. Because of the unusual outcome of the match, even those that might have had winning tickets were afraid that the casino would deny payment to them. Certainly, there were a lot of angry and well-armed patrons.

Then members of the crowd started overturning gaming tables in the middle of the casino at the MGM Grand Hotel and Casino, where the boxing match was held earlier that evening and which was across the street from our hotel. Several violent fights also broke out.

My coworkers and I could hear the sound of gunshots coming from across the street. Then our hotel's security personnel ran by the casino pit, which contained our gaming tables and where I stood, and repeatedly shouted, "Everybody, get under the tables! Now!"

I was dealing cards at the pai gow poker table at the time. Luckily, the last patron had just left my table, and it was now empty. So I just took the cover plate from the table and put it over the rack where the casino's gaming tokens were being stored on my side of the gaming table. With the casino's money secured, I quickly forced myself under the table.

It was certainly an awkward situation at my age. I was already a mature woman. I did not enjoy being forced under the table and all the associated stress. Luckily, I was not overweight; otherwise I could not have even fit in such a cramped space.

How lucky I am! I thought to myself with some sarcasm, for yet again to be a witness to such events.

When security personnel finally gave us the stand-down order, it was fine by me. I stood up. I then saw that some of my coworkers had had to lie down and seek shelter on the dirty floor of the casino. Luckily, nobody got hurt.

Later, my family members told me that I should just change jobs and avoid the casinos altogether.

They were wrong, however. The next time that I encountered an active shooter situation, which happened just a few years later, I was not even inside a casino.

One morning, I woke up earlier than usual from a bad dream. In my dream, a couple of criminals were chasing me, so I had to run up a very long flight of stairs but could not find a place to hide. At that point, I had two choices: face the dangerous criminals at the top of the stairs or jump off from a great height. Either way I knew that I would be hurt or worse.

Luckily, I woke up from my dream. It was my day off. I decided to go about my day as usual. When it came to dreams, I certainly did not hold any superstitions. I was going to do laundry at home. I went to buy laundry detergent at a Sav-on Drugs store that was located near the intersection of Rainbow Boulevard and Flamingo Road in Las Vegas.

I was just exiting the store when a policeman stopped me. I told the policeman that I had paid for everything in my cart, and I showed him my receipt.

"This is not about you," the policeman told me. He called out, "Attention, everyone!" The policeman then started making an announcement. "There is an active shooter at the other side of Flamingo Road, at the hair salon. He has a rifle. Bullets are flying in all directions. Until we clear this area, no one leaves this store."

An old man who was standing next to me broke down in tears. He appeared to be under an immense amount of stress. He started to cry on my shoulder.

"My daughter is a hairstylist at the salon where the shooting is going on," he finally blurted out.

Later, we learned that the shooter was just released from jail. Apparently he had found out that his girlfriend was cheating on him while he was serving time in jail. Of course, this would only be their private business. Yet this criminal wanted to put on a scary show for his girlfriend that the whole world would see.

He caught up with his girlfriend at the hair salon. This insane criminal then lectured her there with his gun in hand. He had already fired off a couple of warning shots to scare her, and by accident, one of his bullets hit someone in the knee who was enjoying a pizza at the pizza parlor next door. The bullet went through the drywall that separated the two businesses. The other shot shattered the glass window of the store. Luckily, the shooter allowed all the workers from the hair salon to leave at the beginning of his rampage.

When he finally heard that his daughter was safe, the old man next to me was happy that she had survived the incident without harm. At that time, I started to grow concerned about my son, who would stop by at my place that evening for a visit. I was worried that if he did not find me at home, he would be worried or upset.

I looked out through the store's glass window in the direction of the hair salon and saw that the police tactical team was still all spread out throughout the lot, taking up various positions behind cars. One of the officers was lying down on the ground with his high-powered rifle behind my new car.

"My God," I said. "My new car will be riddled with bullet holes."

After three hours went by, I could not take it anymore.

I'd better go, I thought to myself.

A few minutes later, I asked the policeman if I might go home because I had the only key to my apartment. I explained to him that my son would be visiting me, would not be able to go in, and might be worried about me when he found my place locked up. My son did not have a cell phone where I could reach him. Cell phones were not so common at that time.

When he heard about my predicament, the policeman was nice to me. By then, the officer in tactical gear, who had initially taken up a position behind my car, had moved to a new location.

"Yes," he said, "you can go home, so long as you take responsibility for what happens to you. When you get in your car, do not turn the lights on. You will need to carefully drive in the opposite direction, away from the scene. Go quickly."

By this time, four hours after the ordeal had begun, the police had already convinced the gunman to surrender. He was just negotiating the terms of his surrender.

When I finally arrived home, my son was there waiting. He told me that my friend Mary had already called him at work. This was after I was able to place a call to Mary earlier from the store to ask her to pick me up. However, Mary could not get me out because the entire area was cordoned off. So, instead, she notified my son about the situation.

"Mom," my son asked me, "how could you go to the only place in this town where there is a shooting going on?"

"Believe me," I said to him, "I was not looking for trouble. I only wanted to buy laundry detergent. Please do not blame me."

Unfortunately, we never know when and how a disaster may strike. A few days later, at my son's workplace, there was yet another shootout in the parking lot of his casino. My son had to look for cover as he exited the employee door of the casino on his way home.

It seems that no matter where we are, we always have to be on guard and be ready to face an unexpected danger. We cannot be safe anywhere, not even in the White House, at least according to some news stories.

Sadly, in some countries, human beings live as prey for the more powerful. In the Middle East, rivers could flow from all the blood of innocents who have been killed by extremists. Not surprisingly, refugees are fleeing such regions by the thousands.

While there may be plenty of such killings in many societies, we have to believe that extremists and murderous individuals can be stopped in most instances. Outrageous crimes can at least be reduced. We have to educate people to appreciate life and also to care about the world that we all live in.

Throughout history, there has always been killing. Sadly, it appears that such thirst for blood is part of human nature. Yet one story about love and empathy has always amazed me.

It was a memorable event that occurred during Christmas 1914 on the battlefield of World War I. There was a series of widespread but unofficial cease-fires along the Western Front. In the week leading up to the holiday, German and British soldiers, who were on opposing sides, crossed trenches to exchange seasonal greetings and to talk.

In some areas, men from both sides ventured into the no-man's-land between the respective front lines on Christmas Eve to mingle and to exchange souvenirs. Several such meetings ended in carol-singing. The Germans sang "Silent Night," and then the English sang "Good King Wenceslas." Some of the men even played games of football with one another, giving one of the most enduring images of the truce.

In the end, the leadership of the two armies made it clear that such fraternizing with the enemy would not be allowed. One English commander came running and ordered back his soldiers. He reminded them that they were there to kill the enemy and not to make friends with them.

The English and German soldiers shook hands, hugged one another, and then returned to their posts. The next day, the fight was on again.

These soldiers knew in their hearts that guns would not solve their problems. The real solution lay with the people in charge. The soldiers knew that their war was not a benefit to anyone—it was not the proper resolution of disagreements. Indeed, great people, such as Mahatma Gandhi, Martin Luther King, and Nelson Mandela, were all able to achieve some of the greatest things for all of humanity without firing a single shot.

Regardless of where we live in this world, we have to care about other people's lives and about our environment. We have to start at home. We should not buy guns as birthday or Christmas presents. Instead, we have to educate our children to respect and value human life; we must teach them that one may use a weapon only in self-defense or in defense of our nation.

Guns can cause not only physical wounds but also invisible wounds that might never heal. Given such broad and irreversible impact, we should, as a society, carefully evaluate all things that are associated with the ownership of guns and appropriately punish all of those who are responsible for the most outrageous crimes.

I am proud to be an American, but like many, I am worried about the future of this country. I am concerned about the fate of our nation the same way that I am concerned about my friends and relatives. Having deranged individuals run wild because of the lack of stronger gun regulations, individuals who are able to cause such great harm to innocents, reflects negatively on us as a nation.

In other countries, such senseless acts of violence in the United States reverberate. In particular, I often hear that "the United States cannot keep order at home; it fails to control its criminals. Therefore, it cannot be taken seriously as a respected leader of the free world."

Yet some of the violent acts do not have anything to do with gun control laws; they are committed by extremists and criminals who have no respect for such laws. Terrorists, especially, are so extreme that neither law nor negotiation can help. They do not follow any laws. As one of my colleagues said, "They need a checkup from the neck up!"

"I am happy that you survived your incident without harm," Mary, my friend, told me following the shooting incident at Sav-on Drugs on Flamingo Road. "I think those people who cut short the lives of others will, in the end, always suffer negative consequences themselves. Either the legal system or the relatives of their victims will catch up with them. Even in those rare cases that they are not apprehended, such bad people often end up with shorter lives or a deadly disease. God is watching over all of us."

We cannot take anything for granted. We have to keep working on good solutions to peaceably live together. With a little more understanding, we could all live more happily without these mass shootings.

CHAPTER 7

INTIMACIES

Finding happy moments and time for laughter makes each day a good day. Once we reach our fifties, we start to integrate our memories. We think often about our past. We recount our earlier activities in life to make sure that we have not missed anything. This process of personal inventory is often painful, because we do not want to remember those things that made us sad or did not turn out so well.

I have a friend who works at a small store. To protect her privacy, I will call her Clara. I usually go to her store to buy small trinkets. Clara is in her sixties and lived in many countries, many beautiful places, with her husband. Her husband is a member of the military.

Clara is a very nice person. She is also a very happy lady, or so I thought until one day, I found her in tears. She is also a big fan of taking personal inventory of past memories and recounting events that happened to her a long time ago, but to my surprise, she was really beside herself on that particular day.

"I hope that my husband will die first, and then I will flush his ashes down the toilet for being an unpleasant and lazy partner for all of these years," she told me. She continued that her husband had been sitting by the computer all day every day, and when she asked for help with anything, he became irritated and critical about things she does or says. According to Clara, he would not even go with her for grocery shopping or to have dinner with her in a nice restaurant. He was also not interested to see a show with her or to go on a vacation with her.

"Why did you marry your husband?" I asked Clara.

"Because my daddy told me to do so, but at that time, things were very different. I lived with my family. I was in love with a German pilot, David. My daddy did not like the Germans, and he asked me to end my relationship with the German pilot. He wanted me to tell David that our feelings were not mutual anymore and I did not love him.

"After I sent David away, I did not hear of him for a long time. A month ago, I received a letter from him, through my relatives who still live in Germany and accidentally found him. During the past thirty-five years, I've thought many times about David, and I felt guilty, because I ended the relationship with him, as my daddy had commanded."

She showed me David's letter and cried. This is what David wrote:

> The memories of our first love and your beautiful face will be with me so long as I live. I am haunted by your face and your words that you do not love me. Did I err when I gave my heart to you? I do not think so. It was probably your father who made you tell me that you did not love me, as he disliked me.
>
> I am still longing for you, and I hope that you think of me with the same passion. When I close my eyes, you are always with me, and I still love you. In case you will be free one day, I want to marry you as much as I wanted to marry you thirty-five years ago.

We cried together over David's letter and his infinite love.

"What do you think? Would David feel the same way today if you had married him all those years ago?" I asked Clara.

"I do not know that for sure," Clara explained, "but I know that he was a gentleman in every way. I should not have listened to my daddy and sent David away."

I then shared with Clara that I married my first love, and he also told me so many nice things, such as, "You are the queen of my heart!" "I will always love you and be at your side!" "I never want to be without you, because you are my everything!" and so on.

Unfortunately, ten years later, I found out that he had been cheating on me most of the time and that he was intimate with other women regularly behind my back. His excuse was that "Variety is the spice of life!" "I need it to manage my stress, although I love only you!"

All of this was very strange to me, because all the while my ex-husband was cheating on me, he would still be very jealous of me. If any man said hello to me, he asked many questions and told me not to smile at any man.

In the end, it was ever more difficult for me to live with my ex-husband. After he slapped me on my face, I divorced him. Life always brings changes, and sometimes it is difficult to deal with these changes, especially if they are not in our favor. I can say this with some experience, as I am now in my sixties.

"If you would be interested in a good funeral parlor," I said jokingly to Clara, who was about the same age as me, "here is one I have for your husband."

I handed her an advertisement that I had just received in my mailbox that I opened on my way to her store. This funeral parlor in Las Vegas had been regularly sending me their proposals for years, with a very detailed price list for various funeral services that they apparently could provide me. One day, I finally got fed up.

In the past, this is what they wrote to me:

Yesterday is history; tomorrow is a mystery.
Today is a gift, and that it is why it is called the present.

Our present is a cremation service that makes your life easier and makes sense, because it is less expensive, it has less impact on the environment, and it allows a dignified resting place for your loved ones to visit.

While they tried their best to keep their advertisements witty and nicely worded, receiving these reminders about their cremation service each month, sometimes even twice a month, with offers of further price reductions, became very irritating to me. At my age, I certainly did not like being constantly reminded of an imminent death. Do they seriously think that I care about how inexpensive and environmentally friendly they are if they regularly remind me that I need to think about my cremation?

So, this is what I wrote back to this funeral parlor/crematory:

Dear Sirs,

Please at once stop sending me your monthly business offers for my funeral. Trust me: I do not want to cremate myself while I am still alive and happy, regardless of your "dignified and economic" offers for my burial.

You surely must work for the devil, because your letters urge people to die before their appointed time so that they can receive your services at "deeply discounted prices."

Your creepy reminders for the last several years, sometimes as often as twice a month, stress me out. They try to rush me to die. Any licensed psychologist would tell you that your letters urging crematory services for the elderly would have a negative effect on their recipient, especially on those who already have health problems and are even more harmed by this type of stress.

My life or death should not be your concern at all, because that is only a concern for God and for my family. Therefore, you should not worry how much impact my dead body will have on the environment or how dignified my remains will be at their final resting place.

If you do not stop harassing me with your letters, I will contact an attorney.

I wish happy cremation to you and to your loved ones.

Zsazsa Anderson

When my friend Clara had read my letter, her tears were still falling but now from laughter. I also shared with her that one of my coworkers' uncle died at this particular crematory of a stroke when he was given a detailed bill for his wife's funeral expenses, because this funeral parlor had charged him even for a glass of water that he drank at his wife's funeral.

In the end, Clara and I had cried together and laughed together, and therefore, it was a good and very refreshing day for both of us after all. Our tears rinsed our eyes to see things more clearly in our own lives and to be able to put things in the right context. Indeed, laughter is the shortest distance between two people and the best cure.

"What can I do?" Clara finally said. "My husband, with our sons, is now more part of my life than David. It seems that I cannot live with my husband, nor can I live without him. That train with my earlier love, David, is now gone forever. It is an unforgettable memory, but I have to be happy with the things that I have now."

"It is good to have family and love, and it is nice to belong to people who care for you," I told Clara. "We are the makers of our own daily happiness. At least, you have nice memories. I think you should talk to your husband more openly; do not let him isolate himself."

CHAPTER 8

THE PERFECT HUSBAND

The following events, which relate to my life with "Mr. Wonderful," remind me of the childhood fairy tale about "The Raven and the Cheese." In the fairy tale, a raven is perched high up in a tree, with a piece of cheese in its beak. It is about to have the cheese for dinner. Just then, a fox happened to run by the tree. The fox saw the raven and its treasure and decided to get the cheese for himself. However, the raven was too high up in the tree for the fox to be able to reach the cheese.

"What a nice day," slyly said the fox to the raven. "It is a real pity that I cannot also hear your beautiful voice. This evening would be even more delightful if you sang us a song."

The fox's compliment took the raven completely off guard. "Oh, yes, yes," said the raven as it started to clear its throat. Indeed, hearing the fox's compliment, the raven's attention was taken away from the piece of cheese in its beak. The raven dropped the cheese. When the raven let the cheese out of its beak, the cheese fell on the ground, where it was quickly devoured by the fox.

Flattery can be a shortcut for some to get what they want. It serves as a kind of music to our ears—pleasuring us, instilling in us a false sense of trust, and sometimes, even leading us to a false world of illusions.

In Las Vegas, it is hard to find a trustworthy man, even with a magnifying glass. A good man, of course, does not have to be perfect. We are all far from perfect. A good man just has to have a sincere desire to love, to care, and to keep his word.

Las Vegas, or Lost Wages as some have called it, is a gaming paradise. It was made for gambling. Indeed, the majority of men here are gamblers.

Gambling addiction is an impulse control disorder. As an addictive behavior, it belongs in the same psychologically deviant group of behaviors as drinking, imbibing illicit drugs, and engaging in high-risk sexual activity.

There are many treatment centers in Las Vegas, as well as elsewhere, to treat addiction, but most choose not to take care of their addiction. Instead, they try to hide it or even deny it to themselves. Even if they realize they have a problem, some of them are afraid that they would be stigmatized if they sought treatment. In other cases, some are just not strong enough or determined enough to make a change.

Societies have a difficult time dealing with sociopaths, albeit at least 20 percent of the prison population is afflicted with these types of personality disorders.

There are many sociopaths in Las Vegas, all of whom live on the edges of the accepted social norms and beyond. Such sociopaths are often heavy drinkers and gamblers. They care less about others. To be exact, they care about others only when they need their help.

Sociopaths do not feel a sense of belonging to any one place or to any one person. Instead, most of the time, they ignore the lives and livelihoods of others around them. In their warped view, empathy is for suckers.

If some of the time persons with such personality disorder exhibit some attachment and encouragement to you, such display of affection is not enough to fully trust them. Sadly, sociopaths do not hesitate to do anything to make their own existence easier—sometimes lies to gain their target's trust and confidence, and at other times, even the use of force.

A recent news report in Las Vegas acknowledged that Las Vegas is not only one of the gaming and entertainment capitals of the world, but it is also one of the human-trafficking capitals of the world as well. Some Las Vegas gangs traffic in kidnapped women and children, who are sold for sexual slavery. In this city, it is important to stay on the lookout for strangers all the time.

Sociopaths search for easy prey, and they are willing to engage in any profitable relationship, regardless of consequences, without hesitation. Of course, it is always easier for us to wise up to such realities once we have had some exposure to them.

Las Vegas is a city that is in a constant state of change, with the exception of most of those who suffer from deviant addictions. Such addictions do not often go away. Some homeless people sleep on the street, but they still live better in Vegas than just about anywhere else. In this city, it is easier to eke out a basic existence, because the weather is warm most of the time, and food can be received for free or for pennies in many places around the city.

Some of the homeless carry sleeping bags and personal signs used for begging. Some of these signs even manage to entertain. One sign said: "I want to work for a beer!"

Las Vegas is perhaps one of the most dynamically developing cities in the United States. Such dynamic development also affects personal relationships and personal objectives; many want to live for today only and not to worry about tomorrow.

On one sunny and hot day in May, I traveled by bus near the Las Vegas Strip, the city's commercial center, because my car was getting repaired. I waited approximately thirty minutes for the bus to arrive. Finally, when the bus did arrive, it was very crowded. The passengers were squeezed together like tuna fish in a can.

Some of the passengers were cursing not only because the bus was so crowded, but also because they had to switch buses earlier. Apparently, the first scheduled bus along this route had broken down somewhere at an earlier stop, and about half of the riders had to wait for a long time in the punishing heat for the next one to come along. So this was the next bus that picked up all the overheated and exhausted stranded passengers, which made for one unhappy and crowded bus ride.

"If you touch my behind again," said one of the older passengers, who was squeezed against another, "I will break your neck and stick your head up your ass."

Then the person next to him responded with even harsher curse words.

Their words made me uncomfortable; luckily, I could sit down a few steps away from them. In the end, all of this still appeared to turn out the best for me, because I found Mr. Wonderful sitting right next to me.

He had blue eyes and dark brown hair. He was handsome and well dressed. He wore a dark blazer and had a friendly smile on his face.

Once I sat down next to him, we engaged in a long conversation. He told me that he moved to Las Vegas just a few weeks ago from Louisiana. He also told me that the police had temporarily impounded his car, because he did not yet have a chance to purchase the required car insurance for Nevada.

"I am going to find a good-paying job first, and then I can take care of my car situation," he explained. "But, to date, I only have promises of a good job."

He also shared that he was married in the past and that, in his prior life, he was a real estate broker. He said that the long hours at the office and the associated work stress made his life miserable. Given all the stress, his wife could not tolerate their life together anymore. One day, during one of their arguments, she had thrown a grilled chicken on their living room wall in a fit of anger. Shortly after this episode, they had decided to divorce.

Mr. Wonderful asked me to have dinner with him. He said that he had received a complimentary dinner ticket from a friend to Hugo's Cellar, which was one of the high-end restaurants at the time, at the Four Queens Resort and Casino.

We met up about a week later. I wanted to give myself time to think over our conversation on the bus. In any event, he was also busy looking for a job, trying to get back his car, and working on settling in the city.

To my surprise, following our meeting, he sent me flowers at the casino every day where I worked as a blackjack dealer. It was very romantic. All my coworkers envied me.

For our date, Mr. Wonderful arrived with a big smile and with even more beautiful flowers.

"Where have you been all my life?" he asked. "You are beautiful inside and out. You are like a spring flower, who is beginning to blossom. I hope that I can see you more in the future."

He made me feel very special. He made me feel really good.

Together, we went to the movies, the Vegas shows, the zoo, and the outdoors. It was all nice and fun. It was nice to have someone who cared for me. It was magical to be loved again.

Three weeks later, my mother arrived to my home from overseas for a short stay. She was happy for me.

"It is better for you to have a nice partner at your side," she said. "You certainly went through a lot. Your life will, hopefully, be a bit easier with him by your side."

My mother liked my future husband, and she cooked delicious Hungarian food for him. In turn, Mr. Wonderful brought home flowers and small gifts for my mother. It was all very nice.

Then, one day, he asked me to marry him.

"I always wanted a woman who is as kind and as understanding as you are," he said. "You remind me of my mom. I promise to be your Mr. Wonderful until the end of our lives."

I said "yes" because I thought that he was Mr. Wonderful and that he loved me. I was certainly very fond of him, ever since that first fateful day that we had met on the bus.

He had an engaging personality for sure. He also had put on a good show for me at the time when I most needed it, because I was lonely. Early on, he showered me with compliments and with flowers all the time.

A few weeks later, after we were married, I received a telephone call from his ex-girlfriend. She said that I'd better watch out for Mr. Wonderful, because things were usually not the way that he liked to describe them. She said that her name was Katrina, but she did not provide any further details. I thought that maybe she was just jealous of me.

"I hope that you make it with him, because I was not smart enough for him," she then said sarcastically to me. "Your husband told me that you are a good homemaker and clean. Now, my best wishes to the both of you!" She then hung up.

I told my girlfriend Mary what Katrina had said on the telephone. She was not surprised. She told me that when she talked earlier with my husband, he did not show too much affection for me.

"She is a good person, and I married her to stay with her," my new husband apparently told Mary.

So, as I learned from Mary, my new husband did not say to her, "I married her because I love her" or "because I am crazy about her." He did not say anything like that. Mary, of course, did not like how he spoke about me.

I thanked Mary for the eye-opening information. Naturally after this, I began to look at my "wonderful" husband more carefully.

I was already beginning to become a little suspicious. My husband had told me that he was not a gambler. He said that he would only very rarely make a tiny bet when his favorite team, the Dallas Cowboys, would play, to make for an even more exciting game.

A few days later, unfortunately, it happened that I washed his jacket in the laundry machine. When he came home, he looked upset. He told me that his winning ticket had been in the inside breast pocket of his jacket.

I felt bad. I paid for his winning bet just to avoid an argument. *I am not an expert on sports betting anyway*, I thought to myself. However, I only later realized the extent of his scheming.

"Do not worry, my little darling," my husband said to me then, "money will come to me from everywhere. My ex-wife owes me half of the value of our old house. My friends also owe me half of the value of my old real estate business.

"You are the goddess of my good fortune, and our home together will be forever our palace," he kept saying.

"I feel very lucky to have a beautiful wife, a handsome stepson, and an ugly cat," he added for comic effect. This was a reference to my son and to my cat. He looked upbeat as he spoke, and all of this sounded nice and somewhat humorous. I later regretted that I did not ask him why it was that he found my cat ugly. His answer probably would have opened my eyes sooner.

Then winter came. My husband was busy working as a driver for a limousine company until one day he was fired.

"I got fired because I misplaced some paperwork," he explained to me. "My paperwork flew out through the open car window, and therefore, I was not able to document to my boss how much money I had made for the company on that day."

As I later learned, this was not the first time that he had less money on hand to provide to the company than his rides should have netted.

Following the loss of this job, things changed rapidly. My husband disappeared each day to look for work. In the evenings, when he returned, he was always in a bad mood. My husband's outlook had turned for the worse for sure. He would slam doors and grind his teeth. He told me many negative things about life. He was especially critical of politicians.

"They are all crooks," he used to say regularly.

One day, a girl called on our home telephone while my husband was away. She said that her name was Gloria and that she was a dancer at one of the gentlemen's clubs. When I tried to find out more, she just hung up the phone. I was, of course, upset by her call.

"What was the real reason for her call?" I asked my husband firmly after I informed him about what had happened.

"Do not be jealous," he said. "She just needed a ride. I helped her because she is very attractive and pays well. Don't you know that variety is the spice of life?"

"Yes," I responded, "I knew that about the food we eat, but I did not know that about your appetite toward other women."

I did not know and did not like finding out about this side of Mr. Wonderful.

In October, he had brought home his winter clothes from his storage unit so that I could launder them and get them ready for the cold season. He told me that he kept his storage unit for junk and things he did not presently need, like out-of-season clothing. He also said that he kept his second suit there. He only wore one suit all the time when he was with me. Apparently, my husband's need for variety did not extend to his wardrobe.

"I need only two suits," he used to tell me jokingly. "One suit I wear with you for celebration of our life, and one suit I am saving in storage for my funeral."

I was not so sure that there even was a second suit. In any event, I began to launder his clothes from storage the next morning while he went to "look for work." To my big surprise, just about each and every item of clothing from the storage had receipts for various bets and wagers that he had placed all around town. Inside his winter jacket alone, I found a big bunch of betting tickets from several different casinos. All of them showed that he had placed wagers on an endless series of different sports teams, on horses, and on everything else for which a wager was legally accepted, except his poor mother's grave.

I counted up all the losing tickets that I could find in his pockets. I found that in a matter of just a few months, he had already lost about $1,200. At the time, this represented about the price of a Hawaiian vacation.

That was a "little bit" more than the very tiny sum or "ten dollars" he told me that he wagered very rarely on his favorite team, the Cowboys. Unfortunately for him, I also found among these tickets the one ticket that he had placed on that important Cowboys game and that he had told me that I accidentally washed away and destroyed in the laundry machine and for which he let me pay his entire winnings. In fact, in researching this particular game, I found that it was not even a winning ticket. He had lied about this ticket to me as well.

Among these papers I also found a tax return for the previous year. In it, he listed his ex-girlfriend, Katrina, as his wife (although he said they were never married), and he also listed Katrina's dog, Jackie, as his dependent.

From his tax return, I could also see that he had already lived in Las Vegas for at least a couple of years, not just for a few short weeks, as he had told me earlier.

Seeing all of this at once, I needed to sit down for a moment and take a deep breath. At first, I thought I might be imagining all of this; I needed a glass of water. Suddenly it became clear that he had tried to fool me with just about everything he had said to me. In truth, he was a big-time gambler and liar, a person who could not be trusted at all.

Sadly, I loved him and trusted him. I thought that there was real love between us. At the time, it was difficult for me to understand his approach. After all, he repeatedly kept telling me that he loved me very much and had waited to find me all his life. It was, of course, not true. Additionally, I realized that, even if I overlooked his lies and misconduct toward me, I could not protect him from himself and could not change him against his will.

I struggled as a single mom for many years to raise my son. After many years of study and work, my son had just been admitted to one of the best universities. I thought that he might need some financial help. I did not want to flush my savings down the toilet so that Mr. Wonderful could wager all around town. I did not need any more hardship as a result of this bad relationship into which I had inadvertently fallen. I earned my living through difficult physical work as a blackjack dealer.

I ended up calling up my mother by telephone. I told her about what had happened and about my husband's gambling addiction.

"I pity him," my mom said. "He could be a normal partner for you without this gambling addiction. Remember Uncle Freddy? He was an alcoholic, and nobody could help him."

"You should pity me, not him," I said to my mom.

"You are still young and healthy," my mom said, "and you do not have any addictions, so you will make it. Tomorrow will be a new day with new opportunities."

The next day I asked my husband if he would consider undergoing therapy and making some changes.

"Yes, when hell freezes over!" my husband responded.

The following day, I told my son about what I had finally pieced together.

"My husband is crazy about gambling," I told my son. "He is also a real bad egg—someone who cares not about others but only himself. Because he is a con artist and a gambling addict, I will divorce him."

"I am so sorry, Mom," my son responded. "Speaking of con men, I have some bad news as well. My friend who borrowed three hundred dollars from me finally gave me a check to pay back his debt. However, I just found out the check was drawn on a closed bank account, and yesterday, he moved to California. In any event, please do not worry, as I will help you and help to pay for half of the cost of your divorce. We should both try to move on and keep smiling, despite such troubles."

That evening, when I returned home, I caught my six-foot-tall husband chasing my cat with the vacuum cleaner. The cat was desperately trying to find a place to hide, but there was no place to hide from my imposing husband. Finally, once I walked in, my terrified cat jumped up into my arms. The poor animal was already sick.

Previously, I could not figure out what was wrong with my poor cat. I had taken him to the animal hospital. The veterinarian told me that my cat had very high levels of stress. The vet also said that the cat's elevated stress had caused him to stop eating. He also often cried like a baby whenever I was with him and my husband showed up next to us.

Having caught my husband in the act, I no longer had to wonder what had been happening to my poor cat. The reason that my cat was sick and traumatized was that Mr. Wonderful terrorized him with the vacuum cleaner whenever I left our home to go to work.

This was the final straw. I told my husband the next morning to leave, because I wanted to divorce him.

"I cannot take it anymore," I told him. "I am fed up with your lies and your animal cruelty."

Then I told him everything that I had figured out about him—even the things he had tried to keep hidden. He left our home without argument, but on his way out, he told me that he would take me to court and take everything I had. Before departing, he even tried to take from me my wedding ring, which I had just paid off myself over several months.

We only lived together six months as husband and wife, but it took me a year and a half to finally be able to divorce him, because he hid from the process server and played games, all of which was calculated to waste my money for even more attorneys' fees.

During our marriage, I cooked, cleaned, and helped him in every way that I could. I really took good care of him. He even borrowed my car for transportation, "only temporarily," as he kept telling me. In the end, I realized that he just wanted to enjoy my help and support so that he could enjoy his gambling addiction uninterrupted. I was like an insurance policy to provide for a basic lifestyle while he gambled all day and night in the casinos.

Then I learned that he ended up going back to his old girlfriend, Katrina, who had called me previously to warn me about him. She still showed friendship to him after I sent him away. She let him live in her home, so that he could have a place to stay while he was looking for work. She loved him too. Sadly, he chose to take advantage of her yet again.

Katrina's sister-in-law died unexpectedly. While Katrina was visiting her brother in Texas to console him about his loss, my ex-husband emptied out Katrina's entire house, including all her valuables. Apparently, later, Mr. Wonderful told the police that he took Katrina's stuff to a pawnshop because he needed the cash for gambling. He explained to the police that he had an uncontrollable gambling addiction.

Luckily, following this episode, I had proof that I was responsible financially and that he was not. This was important because, in court papers, my ex-husband claimed that he paid for everything in our home. Yet I purchased our furniture and my car with my son's help, as well as everything else. The fact that Mr. Wonderful always spent his last penny on gambling showed that he did not buy anything, as he did not have the resources to pay for it.

I was even luckier that he did not put me or my valuables in the pawnshop. We did not have any community property, except for my "pain and suffering."

I was thankful to Katrina because she ended up helping me by telling me about Mr. Wonderful's theft of her belongings when she found out that my ex-husband was trying to use the legal system to also rob me. She gave me a copy of her criminal complaint against my ex-husband so that I could use it in my divorce.

In the end, as my mom and I had observed, my ex-husband was pitiable. He had all the talent to make a good life for himself, but he failed. He failed because he lacked integrity, dependability, and persistence toward a better life.

Mr. Wonderful and those who are made of the same cloth do not care how they destroy other people's lives around them or how they hurt other people's feelings. They just have to follow their own criminal impulses.

In the end, they are destroying their own lives in the process as well, as karmic justice catches up with them. "What goes around comes around," as it is often said.

After all the wonder of our marriage was gone with my husband, I thought that maybe I had been a fool alone for believing in the things that he told me. *Is there any nice man who can be trusted in Las Vegas?* I kept thinking to myself. *It might be that I just kissed the wrong frog, who just was not meant to be the fairy-tale prince in this case.*

"All bad things in life start with the letter 'm,'" one of my coworkers consoled me with a joke, "'m' as in men, misery, menses, moron, manslaughter, and the like."

My coworker's joke had some basis of reality in my case. Perhaps we got married too fast. Often it takes a longer period of time to really get to know somebody. If things look too perfect in the beginning, one must be even more cautious to avoid those unexpected surprises and emotional shocks that can come later if that initial impression turns out to be false.

A real dissonance between our expectations and reality can lead us to frustration and depression. Following my divorce from Mr. Wonderful, I could not trust anyone for a very long time. *They can all go to the moon and back, but I am not going*, I often thought to myself afterward.

"Congratulations, you survived this crazy man!" my girlfriend told me.

In reality, however, my soul still suffered for a long time.

To the present day, I still feel very uncomfortable with too much flattery, because it reminds me of my ex-husband and the fairy tale about the raven and the fox.

Human relationships should be two-way streets. To keep a healthy balance, both partners have to give and take. Even though we are trying hard to find real love, we are still better off without the black magic of a dishonest relationship, no matter how short-lived.

CHAPTER 9

COME ON, BABY, LIGHT MY FIRE!

Late one night, I was watching a CNN special about predatory criminals when my son paid me a visit. He came by my home because my computer broke down and he was going to fix it. He was surprised by my interest in such a difficult-to-watch television program.

"Mom," he said, "how can you sleep after this show? It is at times like these that I regret that I was not born a girl!" He added, "Because then at least I could watch some nice romantic movies with you, instead of you watching this murderous garbage by yourself."

I told him that there was nothing to worry about, because in my earlier life, I had a few encounters with criminals in the court system and in my private life. Perhaps my prior work in the criminal justice system was one of the reasons for my interest. Another was that in my private life, I also sometimes felt like a magnet for trouble, a person who attracted unwanted attention from certain types of criminals.

For example, earlier that afternoon, one of my neighbors put on a performance across from my balcony. It was lucky that I lived upstairs and our units were separated by a large amount of space.

That afternoon, this young man appeared on his balcony across from my balcony. He said "Hi" and smiled at me. Then he opened his overcoat, which revealed that he was naked. He proudly displayed his genitals and waited for my reaction.

Instead of screaming, I continued to water the plants on my balcony.

"Great show!" I said to him. "I hope that the police will like it too. Why, I should go and call them."

Having heard my words, he immediately disappeared.

The CNN special that I was watching that night was about Dennis Lynn Rader, who was also known as the BTK killer. His initials stood for "Bind, Torture, and Kill," which was also Rader's slogan. He managed to keep residents of Wichita, Kansas, in fear for decades.

When he was finally caught, everybody was astonished as to how something like this could happen. By all accounts, he was a good husband, a father of two children, a Boy Scout leader, the president of his church, and a respected compliance officer. However, all these positions and roles were only a mask for him, which gave him a free pass to cruise around and kill for his own sexual gratification.

He not only committed horrific crimes, but he also sought publicity for his wrongdoing.

"I think that I reached a point of my life, with my kids gone, when I felt kind of bored" was his explanation to the police as to the reasons for his horrific acts.

He was an antisocial, narcissistic, sadistic personality, but his disorders did not reach the level of criminal insanity. He knew the consequences of his crimes.

Criminal insanity is a mental defect or disease that makes it impossible for a person to know what he or she is doing; or if he or she does know, to know that what he or she is doing is wrong. A person who is criminally insane will not be punished for his or her crimes.

Dennis Rader, however, was aware of the consequences of his actions, and therefore, he received a prison sentence of 175 years, without the possibility of parole.

I was happy that Rader received his just punishment; however, my happiness only lasted for a short time because, after my son left, I was sleepless most of the night. I remembered having met two characters similar to Rader in my younger years. This CNN special brought up these bad memories. The television show and my own memories were altogether too much for me.

When I was sixteen years old, I lived in the suburbs of Budapest, Hungary, in an area full of large homes, with even larger gardens. One night, I walked home alone from the bus stop through our subdivision following a high school event.

I was a singer in the school's choir, and I really enjoyed it. At the time, I wanted to be an opera singer. People enjoyed my voice when I sang, but my father never liked this career path for me. He told me that voice alone was not enough for a successful career as a female lead singer. He said that I would cry more than sing for reasons that he would only hint at.

It was ten o'clock in the evening. It was raining, and I could not see a single soul out on the street.

I was walking along quickly to our house because I was afraid that someone might follow me from the bus stop. In fact, someone was already following me.

As I later learned, it was a forty-year-old man named Adolph Bartha. He was slowly following me on his bicycle. Suddenly, he stopped at my side and asked my name. I knew I was in trouble, but I pretended that I was not afraid. I just started to walk even faster without answering him.

My hands were cold, my feet did not want to move, and my heart was racing. I was still far away from my house, although at least I was on our street.

Each house in my neighborhood was surrounded by a fenced yard. The only way in was to ring the doorbell at each front gate and hope that someone opened the door to let you in through that gate into their house. I kept wondering which doorbell I should stop at and ring for help to stop the chase. However, if the home owners were all asleep, it would only make my situation worse, as my pursuer would quickly put an end to the chase.

Finally, I reached my family's house and quickly pushed the doorbell at our gate without turning. At that moment, Mr. Bartha put his big hand on my mouth and grabbed me from behind. I kicked backward at his lower leg with the sharp heel of my shoes, which helped me to free myself from his grip. It was then that I saw that his genital was sticking out from his pants. He was ready for action.

He tried to trip me, but could not because of his bicycle. At that moment, my mother, hearing the doorbell, turned on the porch light and opened the front door of the house. My attacker quickly rode away, saying ugly curse words.

I stood there mute. I was white as a ghost.

I told my mother what had happened. The next day, I also told my girlfriend. However, telling my girlfriend was a mistake, because in just a few days, half the neighborhood was talking about what had happened to me.

The court summons in Bartha's case arrived to our home three weeks later. I was called upon to testify against him. By that time, I had learned more about this crazy man. Bartha's hobby was to molest and rape women between the ages of fifteen and sixty-five.

He was a factory worker with a wife and two children. He usually left two hours early to go to work or stayed late at work to give himself time for his adventures.

I felt very embarrassed to be called as a witness against him, but I could credit it all to my girlfriend's loud mouth. I could not avoid it.

On the other hand, it was better that I testified, so that Bartha would be surely convicted and punished, which I also understood and appreciated. So I went to testify. When I came home from the courthouse, my father was very upset.

"How can you be in a criminal case? What did you do?" he asked.

My mom finally told my father what had happened. My father was very conservative and very strict with us. He was an agronomist, who often traveled to faraway places and was unable to be at home to protect us.

"You cannot go to sing in the choir anymore, and you cannot go anywhere alone after seven o'clock in the evening," he told me.

I said "okay," but I did not like his new rules, even though he had serious reasons for them. My father, of course, was only looking out for my safety. Our appearances with the choir usually took place in the evening. It was sad for me that I could not go to sing anymore. I liked to be in the choir, and I enjoyed singing.

The behavior of Rader, as reported by CNN, reminded me of my encounter with Bartha. Luckily, Bartha had not yet killed anyone when the police caught him.

Sociopaths look at women as objects that are to be used solely for their sexual pleasure. They do not care for their victims' feelings. It is similar with serial killers, like Rader, but they go further in that they will kill their victims and even take pleasure in their victims' terror and suffering.

One of Rader's victims was Josephine Otero, a young girl. Rader entered the Oteros' home through a home invasion. Once he strangled young Josephine to the point that she was almost dead, Rader resuscitated her. Then he strangled her again. He kept repeating this so that he could maximize his pleasure and maintain a high level of erotic thrill by being able to strangle the poor girl yet again.

I was lucky that Bartha's acts did not reach Rader's level of violence. I was lucky that Bartha could not even complete what he had contemplated in my case. In the end, the police did catch Bartha in time. However, the memory of the horror of my encounter with Bartha stayed with me for the rest of my life.

My other scary experience in this regard happened in Las Vegas a few years ago. I had a place on Paradise Road at the time. I did not know much about the lack of safety of this particular neighborhood until, one day, a cab driver was robbed and killed in front of the entrance gate of the apartment complex where I lived.

At the time, I worked the swing shift at a casino, from 7:00 p.m. to 3:00 a.m., each night. One night, I was driving home when I recognized that a big green car was following me. I could not stop next to my apartment because I did not want the stalker to figure out where I lived.

Instead, I was circling around the apartment complex in my car when finally one of my neighbors just arrived home at that hour. I rolled down my car window and told them, "Behind me, there is a green car that has been following me for fifteen minutes. I am scared!" Fortunately, my neighbors then escorted me to my apartment and waited until the stalker disappeared.

The next day, the same green car was waiting for me right outside my apartment complex as I was driving to work. Unfortunately, I could not make out the license plate number of the car. This happened more than once.

So eventually, I decided to ask one of my coworkers for help.

"Could you please drive me home?" I asked him. "It will help me to see what this man is up to. He has been following me in his car for days."

"While I drive up behind him," my coworker offered, "you will need to write down his license plate number."

Sure enough, the stranger in his big green car was waiting for me at the entrance of my apartment complex again. However, because I was heading home in my coworker's car, he did not realize that it was me. I then figured out that he knew that I usually arrived home around this time.

This time, we followed him. Unfortunately, he did not have a plate on the back of his car.

For a brief time, he parked his car on the other side of our apartment complex and got out, leaving his car behind. My coworker walked over to his car to see his license plate number in the front.

"This character is no good," my coworker explained once he returned, "because he is hiding his license plate numbers on the front of the car also; all the numbers are damaged on that plate."

"I am lucky that I did not arrive home alone today," I responded.

The following day, I went to the rental office and requested police assistance. Later, the policeman told me that the stalker was visiting his friend from Florida, and he was looking for an easy adventure. Apparently the policeman told the stalker that he should quickly leave Las Vegas. However, I did not feel safe at our place anymore. Two weeks later, I moved away from this apartment complex.

Life is a roller-coaster ride, with many ups and downs. Yet we have to keep our positive outlook. Even when bad things happen, we have to believe that everything is happening for a reason, things will work out, and we will survive.

Perhaps I would not have picked up on the stalker following me had I not watched television programs about sexual predators. Had I lived in such complete ignorance, I would no doubt have easily become his victim. Yet my son was also right that before bedtime is not the best idea to watch these kinds of television programs. In any event, I was lucky more than once, and being informed certainly helped.

CHAPTER 10

I COULD NOT SAY GOOD-BYE TO THIS WORLD

We take our daily lives for granted. We also anticipate good results, hoping that things will turn out the way we always expected. Unfortunately, life is not about who deserves what or getting an outcome that we believe that we should. Circumstances outside our control often play a greater role in the ultimate outcome. My adverse reaction to a prescription drug showed me that this can be the case.

It happened at the time that my son was moving to Boston. I went to the doctor for a routine checkup.

"You have a low-acting thyroid," my doctor counseled me. "You have to take a pill every day for this problem, and you will need to start right away!"

The thyroid secretes several hormones, collectively called thyroid hormones. Thyroid hormones act throughout the body, influencing metabolism, growth and development, and body temperature. The thyroid plays a critical role in the functioning of our bodies.

High levels of stress, untreated infectious diseases, as well as some other diseases can impair its normal function, as I learned after my diagnosis. My doctor explained to me that a long-term thyroid problem can have many negative effects on our bodies, and as such, ongoing treatment is a must. At the time, I also had an infection, for which he prescribed an antibiotic.

Following my visit with my doctor, I went to the pharmacy to pick up the prescribed medications: sixty-microgram tablets of Armour Thyroid for my thyroid problem, and five-hundred-milligram tablets of Cipro for my mild infection.

However, when I took these prescribed pills together, the effect on my health was devastating. This day was one of the worst days of my life, except for that time that I received news that my mom had passed away. These medications in combination gave me an extremely serious adverse reaction, which almost killed me. All of this happened very quickly as well.

Childbirth was the first time that I had a near-death experience. My baby lay sideways at the top of the birth canal, and an unqualified nurse, without a doctor's supervision, tried to rush along the procedure with drugs, with almost disastrous consequences. At the time, my baby had to be turned in the right direction with the doctor's help. The nurse, however, was in a rush, so my baby and I almost died. All of this happened a long time ago, and it does not give me pain anymore, especially because I got a good son. At least, I got something good out of my misery.

However, not much good came about as a result of my adverse reaction incident. I took the pills that the primary care physician prescribed, which almost permanently cured me of all troubles of life. On a more serious note, life, of course, is very precious, and the final outcome was positive thanks to God and to the people around me.

As I later learned, the dosage of the prescribed medications that I took would have been enough for a horse; for me they were surely more than enough. Having taken the drugs, I could barely take a breath. I also could not drink or eat, because my glandular system had swollen up enormously. I could not speak.

I had the feeling that I was going to die because of the extreme chest pain that I was also experiencing at the time. It was as if my heart was being squeezed by a tiny iron cage.

In this terrible condition, I had to drive myself back to the medical center. At the time, I could barely whisper in the doctor's ear the type of medication that I was prescribed and had taken. My attending physician then immediately called the first doctor who had prescribed those drugs that I had just taken. I could hear them talking.

"You should have only prescribed five micrograms of Synthroid first, and not sixty micrograms of Armour Thyroid, for an allergic patient," my attending physician admonished the first doctor, "Come over to see her. She can hardly speak, and her system is shutting down."

The doctors could not do anything for me at that moment. I was beyond help. They just waited to see if my heart was going to stop or not. Medical staff were getting their equipment ready to resuscitate me in case such an event took place.

They were scared to give me an antiallergy medication because of my shaky condition. They felt that it was risky even to try to give me an antiallergy injection, such as Benadryl, because it could have had unpredictable consequences. They even brought in an oxygen mask, but they did not use it. They examined my pulse every couple of minutes and gave me a bottle of water to drink, which I was unable to do.

I was lying on the medical table and prayed, "Please help me, God. Please do not let me die. My son still needs my help with his schooling."

The doctor called my son, who came right away.

"Mom," he said, "you know that you are strong and I love you very much."

Adverse reactions are the most common type of medical injuries. Such incidents occur every twenty minutes in the United States. About two hundred fifty thousand people die each year from medical mistakes, of which number about one hundred thousand people die each year from adverse reactions to prescription drugs.

Our lack of risk awareness can make an adverse reaction unanticipated—an unexpected enemy. In an episode of adverse reaction, genetic factors, comorbid disease states, and synergistic effects either by and between a drug and the patent's disease or by and between two drugs interacting can all play a role.

Also part of the problem is that existing animal experiments do not always serve as an adequate predictor of a new drug's side effects. When scientists experiment on animals to create new types of medications, their results can be skewed due to the fact that the gestational clock of most animals is shorter than in humans. As such, new drugs sometimes can affect people differently and more severely, even though the Food and Drug Administration has approved the underlying animal trials.

In cases where the potential side effects of a medication could be worse than the disease they are trying to cure, doctors should not prescribe it. Indeed, what happened to me could happen to anyone.

I was lucky that I did not have a cardiac arrest. My son took me home safely. He then called my brother in Hungary, who is a doctor. He listened to my son telling him what had happened. After my brother had expressed heartfelt empathy for my condition, he told my son to put me on the phone.

"Do not panic," my brother said. "They poisoned you with the wrong medication. It was also an instance of overdose. We all feel for you, but please try to be strong. Do not worry about your symptoms, but make sure that you do not take any further medications because even a small amount of new chemicals in your system could even further throw off your body's balance. Our body naturally regulates and rearranges itself back to normal. Drink plenty of water, try to eat yogurt, and if you're really hungry, only eat bland, low-fat, low-fiber foods. Unfortunately, your stomach will now be a problem for a longer time period. In some cases like this, the stomach may take six months to fully heal. Most importantly, please keep repeating to yourself daily, 'I am not sick!'"

Following the first day, I had terrible chest pain each and every day, as if someone were trying to press the air out of my lungs. I called my brother again, who told me that I could try to take half of a nitroglycerin pill, placing it under my tongue. I had a few pills that my mother had left during her last visit.

I still remember what some young people at the casino where I worked advised me to do when I returned to work. They said that I should drink Red Bull, which is a drink with caffeine and other stimulants, which they said would rearrange my heart rate at once. However, such sudden change and increased heart rate for someone in my condition could be deadly.

"Red Bull would cure you," they kept telling me. "You should have one every day."

I remember that some of them would drink that stuff all night long, in combination with alcoholic beverages. I never had one, fearing the risks in my condition. I felt that it was not a good idea to play games with increasing my heart rate. It was difficult enough for someone in my condition at the time to endure the regular stressors associated with my work.

In any event, I could not work for the first three weeks after my adverse reaction. On a daily basis, I felt the closeness of my death, as I had terrible chest and stomach pain. My son stood at my side in his free time and tried to comfort me.

"You are going to be all right," he would say. "I love you very much, and I need you. You should keep saying to yourself, 'I am okay; I am not sick.'"

"Yes," I would respond, "if I could at least catch my breath."

At the time, I also visited a store that sold herbal supplements to look for some kind of antioxidant tea. I thought that drinking such tea might help to restore my insides sooner. One of the salesgirls told me that she had a cardiac arrest from a similar incident with prescribed medication. She told me that she was lucky that she lived near a hospital at the time; otherwise, she would have died. She told me that it was best for me not to drink any tea either—the safest drink was only water. She said that if I drank something else, I might have another unexpected chemical reaction.

I called my brother again before I returned to work to thank him for his support and advice.

"I am very grateful to you," I told him. "I do not think that fate has treated me fairly. I got this problem just when my son needed me the most because he was moving to Boston to continue his studies."

"We can find fairness only in fairy tales," my brother responded, "and even in fairy tales, only the youngest son will find it, and only at the end of his long and arduous journey. For fairness in life, we have to fight and negotiate most of the time. Fairness will rarely come without struggle. We always have to be on guard. I think that you are very lucky and strong that you survived this adverse reaction and overdose incident. Be happy. I always say to myself, 'That which does not kill us makes us stronger.'"

I realized that what he had said was very true. My survival was hanging by a very thin thread for weeks. However, in the end, I did survive; my body overcame all the negative effects of the overdose and adverse reaction caused by these drugs.

Three weeks after my poisoning, I went back to the casino to work. I looked like a ghost. My skin was still pale. My breathing was still uneven from the pain that I was still experiencing in my chest. The other table-game dealers started a collection for my benefit. It was a very kind gesture. They all showed their deep empathy for me.

I tried my best to do my job, but I could not perform it with the speed with which they wanted me to perform it. Thus, casino management put me on a Big Six game, because this is a table game on which there is usually a lot less to do.

My son and I were only three months away from a move to Boston, where my son had been admitted to a prestigious university. Given all the things we intended to move with us, we had to undertake a cross-country drive from Las Vegas to Boston with a big truck.

I did not agree with him that he should go alone and live in a dormitory. Anything could happen. I would be thousands of miles away. At this time, there were many negative news stories about dormitories, as well as about fraternities and their initiation practices. I really wanted to be at least in the same town, so that I could help him.

Yet I was worried about our future and about the high cost of my son's tuition, in addition to all the other associated expenses. Then I received a letter from our old friend Albert, who lived in Germany.

I had known Albert for twenty-five years at that time. We had corresponded off and on. Albert was the head of a sports association near Nuremberg. Albert and members of his sports association had visited my old country, Hungary, as part of a tour group a few years before I had moved to the United States.

At the time, I worked as a tour guide in Budapest, Hungary, for international groups, who were mostly from Germany and Austria. It was only during the summers, while there was a summer recess at my university, that I would work as a tour guide. Albert was part of one such tour group.

Albert's German sports association liked me right away for being friendly and informative. The fact that I spoke their language fluently helped. The fact that I was also able to sing with them all their favorite German folk songs on their bus as we visited different sights in Hungary was of course even better. I had learned these German folk songs in high school, which had special German instruction.

When Albert found out about my difficult time with my adverse reaction to the medication and about my son's admission to a prestigious and expensive university, he wrote me a long letter. In his letter, he also included a check for $6,000, which was a lot of money at the time.

"I send this to you for your son's education," he wrote. "Please do not worry about giving it back. I have more than enough money.

In fact, some of this money comes from our sports association. You can pay it back only if you would later become a millionaire."

I broke down in tears because of Albert's love and empathy for us. Albert's help came at the best possible time. I could hardly believe it. I was very thankful.

A few weeks later, I visited other doctors, because some of my symptoms still persisted on a daily basis. The new doctors prescribed for my symptoms all kinds of new medications, from Prilosec to bone hormone pills.

At the time, I started to read the detailed prescription descriptions provided by the drugs' manufacturers. Having read them, I decided not to take any of the new medications. Almost all were too strong or potentially dangerous for me. I also remembered my brother's advice.

Some medications stay in our body for several weeks, even after we stop taking them. This is called their second life. There are medications that can cause irregular heartbeat, high blood pressure, diabetes, blindness, internal bleeding, dementia, hormone deficiency, stroke, and also death. Often we do not realize these potential side effects until it is too late.

We rely on doctors, but, sadly, some of them are not fully knowledgeable regarding certain drug interactions. It also happens that sometimes patients forget to tell their doctors about allergies or other drugs that they are taking. It is very important to read the detailed prescription description provided by the drug's manufacturer.

As panicked as I was at the time, I may have even agreed to take other medications had it not been for my brother's good advice. It was a good thing that I did not, or I might already be gone. The only treatment or procedure that I was still willing to allow was an upper gastrointestinal endoscopy, because I never had one and the doctors strongly advised me to have it done.

"What was the reason," my girlfriend asked, "that the doctor had to look down into your stomach?"

"I am not sure," I responded, "but it was only burned tissue that he found. Apparently, a common consequence of overdosing on medication. Of course, it could have been anything else too."

"Of course," my girlfriend responded, "the doc had to look down into your stomach for his money."

We had a good laugh about it. So in the end, I was able to find some humor in my situation. Thank God and the nice people around me, I did survive all of this, even though I was really close to my death. This was a very painful experience for me.

I feel that doctors should be more focused on the side effects of medications, especially taking into careful account each patient's allergies and genetic makeup. Sadly, many doctors have such a heavy workload that they simply do not have time for a detailed analytical diagnosis. Usually, doctors only treat the symptoms and not the patient. Even more troubling, some doctors do not have adequate information about the side effects of some medications, as there are too many medications that are available on the market.

Yet patients often blindly trust their doctors, viewing their doctor as an authority figure. They tend to believe in their doctors fully, as if their doctor were God. Many of them never question anything that their doctor recommends, although their bodies and health are clearly on the line.

"It is very lucky," my son told me, "that the Internet now has all the important information about drugs, clinics, and doctors. The next time, before undertaking any treatment, we should look into what the Internet provides about the doctor, treatment, and medications."

I agreed with him. We also need to remember that doctors are only human. They can make errors too, and therefore, it is better to be more cautious. It is important to collect more information. In case we face complicated health problems or surgery, we had better seek a second opinion. The Internet is also a good source for finding out about a doctor's malpractice cases. My girlfriend Mary told me that she saw on CNN a news story that one doctor prescribed chemotherapy for several years for thousands of his patients who did not even have cancer.

We have only one life to live. There are certain actions, especially when it comes to our health, that can result in consequences that are permanently irreversible. We cannot take anything for granted in our lives. We have to remember that our health and reasonable mind are our most precious possessions. We must never let down our guard. When it comes to medical treatment, our alertness is very important in avoiding potentially devastating effects on our health.

CHAPTER 11

SWEET LUELLA

Her name was Luella. She was a twenty-three-year-old girl from Argentina. She was attractive, blond, slim, and soft-spoken; her main focuses were art and dress fashion. On the other hand, she was haughty and somewhat conceited, with a touch of a narcissistic attitude. She arrived with her girlfriend, Nana, from Argentina to practice the language and, most importantly, to find a husband.

She was the girl who most impressed general surgeon Thomas Keaton; that is what he thought after a few dates with Luella. No matter what this girl did and how strange she sometimes acted, Thomas adored her.

At first, love was not really important for Luella in her marriage with Thomas. Her relationship with Thomas did not look like a match made in heaven, because she did not show any signs of appreciation toward him. She wanted a more romantic-type partner than Thomas. Originally, Luella wanted someone with whom she could dream together, someone who was more romantic and less job oriented than the doctor.

Thomas was handsome, talented, and kind, and he could have had any woman, but he was a professional, more realistic type. Despite the differences, he cared only for Luella because that was love at first sight for him. He liked her youthful appearance, her ballerina look, and her logical thinking, and he did not care about the rest. Luella was about fifteen years younger than the doctor.

Thomas told his mother, "Let me introduce her to you because she will be your relative too. She is my kind of girl."

Carol's first impression about Luella was pleasant. She acted like a little kitten, who did not know anything about the big wide world. For sure, Thomas's mother, Carol, would agree with her son—even if he were to introduce the dragon's daughter herself.

If she is good for my son, she has to be okay for me too, Carol thought. *He is my only son, and I would like to see him happy.* She worried only about the age difference. She told Thomas, "I do not really care about the look of a person as long as she is well shaped and clean. My main concern is that the person you are going to marry will love you. The good look may be pleasant for adventures, but to marry someone, they need more than to look good."

Three months after their first date, they married, and Luella cried because her mother from Argentina could not be present at their wedding. She did not even want to have a celebration dinner with Thomas's family and friends; instead, she went to work.

Carol understood her tears, but she felt by her actions that Luella did not demonstrate any love toward her son or respect for the others.

She told Luella to put makeup on her face to cover the tears because the pictures would show that maybe she was not too happy and the family members and friends would wonder what was happening and make fun of the wedding.

Luella said, "You put makeup on and make up the pictures if that is important for you."

Carol said, "I thought I raised a good son; therefore, any girl would be happy to marry Thomas, but it looks like you are not. I do not feel too good about your manner."

Luella's manner was for Carol a negative warning sign about her future actions.

After the marriage, there were quite a few differences between the young couple and family members.

Luella started with her wish list and wanted a little dog. She did not care about Thomas's warning that they were buying trouble with a small animal. They did not take the time to tame the dog, and it was running in the house and around the house. Thomas found the dog very annoying. The dog left its poop everywhere while he was running up and down the stairs in their home. Luella did not like to clean up after the dog; therefore, Thomas did. On top of everything, the dog wanted to sleep with Luella. It seemed that Luella preferred to sleep with the dog instead of Thomas on their honeymoon.

Her excuse was that the dog was helpless and barking half the day, while Thomas was quiet. All the neighbors complained about the dog, and the home-owner association sent out a penalty of $500. The dog had cost about the same amount, and in the end, Thomas needed to donate the pet for free to one of their friends. After they gave away the dog, Luella did not want to hear about it, because she liked the cute little dog, and to mention it would be a reminder of her errors.

Luella also wanted to get pregnant immediately, against Thomas's request that they travel and learn more about each other first. After six months of her pregnancy, Luella went home to Argentina because she wanted to deliver her first child with her mother at her side. Thomas lived for a year alone; he was sad that Luella chose her mother's company over his when the first baby was born.

Thomas's mother took care of his household, and she did the cleaning and cooking while Luella was in Argentina. Thomas asked his mother to clean at least two times and also with bleach to make sure that their baby would have everything superclean. Carol did it willingly for her grandson, and she was happy to see her grandson when he and Luella returned.

She told Thomas, "Do not be upset with her, because she is new here; most probably she was scared about the childbirth."

Luella arrived back from Argentina with a sweet baby, a small suitcase, and an unhappy face. It was hard to figure out her manner. In a few years, she'd gotten everything any woman could want during ten years of marriage, although she gave Thomas and his mother a lot of hard times.

Sadly, appreciation of Carol's cleaning and cooking was not Luella's forte.

She let the child run around without diapers. She cared little about Carol's great cooking and didn't care for her at all.

Carol told Thomas that at least he should redirect his wife regarding her manner and the household mess, but Thomas said, "She will learn her role with time; I do not want to hurt her feelings. Please do not say anything to her."

Before the marriage, Luella had worked as a hostess during her summer vacation in an Italian restaurant next to Thomas's workplace. After they met, they saw each other every day, and on their days off, they traveled to California tourist destinations.

It seemed they were happy together. Thomas liked Luella's refreshing company and appearance and her quick, practical thinking.

Carol was hopeful that things would work out, although she found Luella selfish and often unconcerned, mostly unrealistic with her expectations.

After many negative experiences about Luella's actions toward Thomas's continuous benevolence, Carol felt as if her son was not appreciated and not really loved.

Luella was a calculating person for her age, but Thomas did not recognize her negative side. He was blinded by his love and admiration toward her. He couldn't have cared less whether she cooked or not, if she cleaned or not, or what she was spending his money for.

A few years after the second baby, Luella had half of a big house, a car, and a lot of nice things. She also went back to school to renew her diploma. She also pursued citizenship, which for some people takes between ten and twenty years to get and always requires a lot of paperwork. Thomas took care of everything.

Luella visited her mother every two years in Argentina, and her mother arrived here every other year for six months. That also happened on Thomas's money and time.

We can never be sure that the doctor got what he was looking for in his life in return for the many positive things he did for Luella and for their marriage.

To make Luella happy, Thomas also took out a life insurance policy on her.

Thomas now had a wife who was messy in the household. Her cooking was often only halfway done and superficial; her baking was okay, though, as long as she did not forget to put sugar in the pastry.

The worst ideas she had in child raising were in her daily disciplines and eating habits. She breastfed Rolland more often and longer than she should have. She had a good excuse for that: "They do not teach how to be a parent in schools." Her mouth was always running on about her own greatness, and she had dozens of excuses for her mistakes. She argued about everything her husband did not do right away according to her expectations and also according to her plans for the future. Thomas never had a dull moment with his wife. He had many stressful moments, but he overlooked everything for Luella's sake.

Unfortunately, none of Thomas's efforts impressed Luella. She could say only negative things behind Thomas's back; for example, "He is eating a sandwich—not my cooking—and setting a bad example for our baby. He is buying things on sale instead of saving money for the children. He should keep his opinion to himself and hold back everything at his work as well. He should not put hairstyling gel on before he goes to sleep." And so on.

Luella was usually cheeky-sharp with her husband's mother, who did not like to listen to her complaints daily about silly stuff. Luella would never take any good advice from Carol anyway because Luella thought that she knew everything.

Grandmother Carol told Luella, "Do not let your son run without shoes on the playground, because people drop anything there, from glass to needles."

Luella did not listen, and her son's toe got cut twice because something stuck in it.

After this, she told Carol, "Do not think I don't want the best for my baby." She managed to say it with a straight face, although the accident happened because the baby walked barefoot in the park.

This was not the only mistake she made in her child raising; there were many others. For instance, she told Grandma Carol that she could not explain anything to her grandson because she, as his mother, got to do it. It seemed that Grandma, with her university and other trainings plus forty years of experience, was not good enough to explain anything to her grandson, Rolland.

Luella told Carol not to use the word *stupid* in the presence of the child. At the same time, Rolland already knew the word; he had learned it in kindergarten.

She told Carol not to buy any toys or gifts, but at the same time, Luella brought home daily gifts for Rolland. In a few years, Rolland had more toys in his room than Toys "R" Us stores.

Carol felt like Luella wanted to alienate her from the family, and no matter how much she helped and tried to even their road for better days, Luella never was satisfied with her.

Luella regularly left the garbage behind the entrance door and the dirty dishes in the sink until Carol explained to Thomas that showed disrespect to her because she was the grandma and the babysitter, not the cleaning lady.

She occasionally cooked and cleaned around her grandson, but she never even got thanks from Luella for the help.

One day Rolland told his mother that his stomach was hurting. Of course, Luella believed it. She believed her son's diagnosis right away although he'd made it up.

Thomas called and said, "Mom, hurry up and please take Rolland to the doctor because his stomach hurts."

Both parents were at work, so Carol asked Rolland, "Where is your stomach pain?"

Rolland pointed toward his chest and smiled. That was already suspicious to Carol.

She tested her three-year-old grandson and asked, "Would you like to eat a little chicken soup with me?"

Rolland said, "Yes, I would," and he ate a bowl of soup like nothing was wrong.

Carol asked Rolland, "Would you like a few strawberries? I brought some nice, fresh ones."

Rolland answered, "Oh yes, yes."

Grandma Carol asked Rolland, "Why did you tell your mother that your stomach hurt? You could not eat if that were true."

Rolland said, "I was just joking with Mama because I did not want to go to kindergarten today."

Grandmother said, "That was a silly idea because your parents now have headaches, and they are sad at their workplaces that you have stomach pain. The money we would pay for the doctor visit would be better spent for strawberries or toys. You also could have medication for no reason. Luckily you told me the truth. We have to call your parents, and you have to tell them that you were joking."

Rolland did it nicely and apologized.

Luella never thanked Carol for finding out the fib; it was like it was not a big deal.

Thomas's mother helped Luella get a job as a waitress in a big Italian restaurant because she said that they did not even find her application when she went back asking for the job. Carol went to the manager secretly to surprise Luella; she told her son. She added, "Luella never said thank you for that either, although the manager had inform her that I asked to help Luella to get this job."

Instead, she said to her mother-in-law, "I did not come here to collect dirty dishes after other people; I have a diploma from hotel management."

Carol answered, "You should be happy that you have a job, because with this high unemployment rate we have these days, many American families are jobless. Also, you can study here later, but your top priority should maybe be your child and the language. By the way, restaurants are the best places for training because you can quickly learn about other people and their human styles, as well as practice the language. When they recognize that you are educated, they will make you assistant manager."

Thomas's mother was right, and six months later, Luella got the assistant manager position. This position gave her too much stress, though, so she did it only a short time and she did not like it. She wanted a bartender job instead for more money and less responsibility.

Luella did not like her mother-in-law babysitting in general because she was too strict and critical by her measures. She told her, "With your strict style, you should go to work for the military."

Eventually Luella started to like her mother-in-law's cooking and her jewelry-making talent, but not her critical style.

To show her talent and to introduce her better side to Thomas, Luella started to make flower arrangements for sale. There were too many different kinds of knickknacks for sale in this country and therefore her business never really prospered, but Luella made a little money with her flower arrangements.

Thomas opened up a website for her to advertise her different flower creations. With Thomas's help Luella started to have a better attitude toward things, but she often made mistakes, and she did not like to say "sorry" for any of her mistakes.

She also judged people by her first impressions, not by longer experiences.

On one occasion when her mother-in-law arrived, they had lunch with her three-year-old son, and Rolland said to his grandmother, "Why did you come here? Don't you see that we are eating and you just bother us?"

Carol came to babysit and brought food for them. Luella did not reprimand her son; instead, she smiled, as if she'd heard a good joke, and started a seminar about language differences.

Carol said, "I do not need a language seminar; a simple apology will do. My grandson should learn to respect other people, especially his grandmother, who always helps."

All of the advice was useless for Luella. She kept making mistakes in child raising, in the household, and also in the treatment of her husband. She did not really care if her husband even had time for rest or sleep at night because of his high stress and her many expectations. No, she felt the husband should do everything: watch the children, wash the dishes, cook, buy the groceries, entertain the family on excursions, and so on.

After Thomas got high stomach acid, Luella told Thomas's mother, "Your son could always say no, but he never did."

Carol answered, "He knows your expectations and does not want to disappoint you in any way. Maybe you could watch out for him a little bit more. He works too hard."

Whereas Luella was not really concerned about her husband's well-being, she made sure that her needs were fulfilled and her mother would arrive every other year from Argentina and stay for six months because she was worried about her own time. She did not like the household and hard work. She wanted to go to school, shopping, and exercising with her girlfriend instead of worrying over the household. She wanted her mother's help.

The top priority should have been her family life and the household, but she did not think so.

She probably thought that she was young and she should have a mate. She took advantage of her husband, who was fifteen years older and very generous. She acted most of the time as if she did Thomas a favor to marry him.

Thomas never complained, not even about his mother-in-law's visit. Instead, he said, "Maybe we will have less stress. The good outcome from Luella's mother's visit is that I have less to worry about the children."

Of course, Luella was happy that she could drop all her household work on her mother's shoulders so she did not have to care about it. She said, "It is bad enough that I have to work in the restaurant and study; I will not waste my time with cooking and the household. My mom likes these things, and therefore it is better that she come and help."

Amazingly, she was not a Goody Two-shoes with her mother either. Her mom was very understanding and helpful, but Luella did not listen to her advice either, which made Carol feel a little bit better. Luella made her mom cry several times, as Thomas told his mother to cheer her up about Luella's rough manner toward her.

Their marriage was not flawless even at the beginning, but unfortunately, it got worse. Luella was upset that her husband exercised some criticism over her child raising and the hygiene level around the house. She breast-fed the child until he was one and a half years old, and he got bad teeth. Thomas bought her a book about child raising, but she ignored it. The dentist service cost Thomas $3,000.

Luella did not like to cook every day, so occasionally she kept cooked food for more than a week in the refrigerator.

Carol threw out the food secretly because she was afraid that they would be sick from it, and she cooked fresh food.

Luella's excuse was that she did not like to waste the food.

Carol thought *Maybe she does not like to cook at all.*

Unexpectedly, Luella kidnapped Rolland after Christmas, while her husband, Thomas, worked. Before that, Thomas had bought a lot of gifts for Luella and her mother, who visited for the holidays, and decorated the whole house very beautifully for them. Thomas's mom cooked and delivered food to the celebration at Christmas.

All of these things did not seem to matter for Luella, and because she got into some kind of argument with Thomas earlier, or maybe because the dentist left a message that their child had bad teeth, she flew home to Argentina with everything, the baby and the gifts also.

Again, she did not consider Thomas's feelings nor the baby's interest. Now the baby needed to cross the world over the ocean a second time. Grandma Carol was not an issue either.

This situation was really sad for Thomas and for Carol.

After six months of separation and disappointment for Thomas, sweet Luella returned with her expectations again. She never asked how Thomas felt; she just came back.

Before that happened, Thomas was very sad. He was often in tears, almost suicidal, over Luella's action, and he kept saying, "I will never see my son again. Last evening, he called me, 'Papa,' and I was very happy."

Thomas's mother, Carol, said, "Luella's behavior reminds me of the story of the scorpion and the frog. The frog delivered the scorpion to the other side of the river, but the scorpion stung the frog instead of saying thank you. The frog asked, 'Why did you do it?' The scorpion answered: 'That is my nature.'"

Thomas answered, "Believe me, I did my best for this girl, but it was not enough for her."

Carol told her son, "Luella did not get enough life experiences yet to think about her actions' consequences. Cheer up; life is difficult in Argentina, so she will most likely return. Believe me, our life is about changes, and you will have the opportunity to meet with them again. If nothing else, she is going to look for your child support."

Luella's action was called "kidnapping of a minor" in the United States, but she couldn't have cared less about it. Her husband's feelings or health were not much of an issue for Luella either, and her mother-in-law's, even less. Carol raised a good son, but Luella did not care for Carol. She never apologized for any of her bad behavior either. The most she once said was, "I did not mean my action seriously"—and that was all she said.

Thomas took Luella back against the odds and all his friends' advice. They all stood at his side while he got the hard times by Luella's actions. Thomas truly loved Luella and his son and tried to build up a relationship with her again. Thomas's mother let her son choose anyone and tried to stay out of their discussions, although she had several negative experiences with Luella as well.

The only thing she said, like all the other friends also, was, "Be careful, Thomas, because if somebody violates your trust, she cannot be fully trusted anymore. You have to keep your eye on her and train her. I would like to see you happy."

Many months went by, and Luella was not satisfied yet. She wanted to have more security for herself, and pleasure for Thomas so she chose to have another child. After that, she seemed to be happy with Thomas, but Luella soon had more plans for her future.

Per his wife's wishes, Thomas did buy a house with her. That meant he put his money down, and half of the property went into Luella's name.

Everybody would think that was already more than generous after her earlier bad behavior, but not Luella.

She also wanted Thomas to renew the house and she wanted to go back to school, while applying for citizenship during the time Thomas changed his job because his earlier workplace closed down for reconstruction. Now they needed to move with their children.

She also wanted to invite her mother every other year to stay for six months. All these things created more obligations for Thomas and emptied his pockets.

One time Thomas said, "It seems I have endless obligations in my life. If that's how it goes, I will have a heart attack shortly. My life with her is like the fisherman's situation with the golden fish. I can never do enough for her."

His words made Carol really sad, and she also felt pain for her own treatment by Luella.

Thomas borrowed money occasionally from Carol, but that did not bother Luella. She always got what she wanted because Thomas loved her, tried to keep the family together, and tried to keep Luella's interest on their marriage.

At the same time, when Thomas's mother needed help around the house, she just handled things on her own or occasionally asked the neighbor to help. It was the same with the money; she would rather go back to work for her old age than ask for money from Thomas because Luella tied up her son to the top of his head with financial and other obligations.

Carol thought, *In his leftover time, my son just needs to breathe.*

That Luella's plans were in a short period of time maybe too ambitious or their family life could be jeopardized with a newborn child did not even cross her mind.

Everybody else recognized that she wanted too much too soon, but not her.

She never asked; she issued marching orders. This way her husband, Thomas, could never oppose anything. He would give it all willingly until he dropped dead because he loved his two children and the idea that he had a young wife.

For Thomas this marriage was, "Till death do us part."

He had too much stress, but he tried to ignore it. High blood pressure, high cholesterol, and high stomach acid are precursors for a heart attack or stroke, but Luella was most of the time "the queen of reluctant" about these things. She did not worry too much about Thomas's health with the life insurance in her hands.

Thomas hoped that his wife would change with time and adapt more easily to situations even if she did not have advantages out of them.

Thomas told his mother, "Anyway, why should we be concerned too much about tomorrow? We should live only for today."

Thomas was happy that Luella loved his beautiful children and had ambitious plans for herself.

He told Carol, "She is fun to be with; she is not visiting bars or using drugs. She is doing fairly enough. What the heck? We aren't all perfect. At least my children are nice and smart."

Thomas's mother had a different opinion about these things. She thought, *Luella wanted too many things too soon on other people's accounts. Luella's manner was selfish and unconcerned. With the children she showed foolish affection and did not care enough about their eating habits or manners. She let them govern themselves, although they were too young for that. At the same time, if anyone tried to redirect them, even Thomas, she got upset. She likes them if they do whatever they want or what she wants; other people do not count.*

To choose the right parenting style was not on Luella's mind; maybe she did not know about parenting. Of course, she probably tried her best but often failed. To choose the right style, first she needed to learn more about these.

Based on psychological perspectives, the parenting styles are authoritarian, authoritative, permissive, and uninvolved. Luella's style was permissive. She made only a few demands on her children, and she was overly responsive to their desires and let them do as they pleased.

She often said, "They are too young, too small, to understand or behave well."

After she had a second child, she was even more often overwhelmed by their daily activities and manners. Probably she did not know enough to follow the right style, and that did not help; instead, it led to certain consequences.

The authoritative parenting style seems to have the most positive effect on a child's cognitive and social development. That means parents are demanding but set rational limits for their children and have close communication with them.

Luckily their son Rolland was very observant and smart for his age; only his discipline by Luella was a failure, and this was more often at home.

Thomas's mother, Carol, was upset about all the understandable reasons, and she was also afraid that the situation would get worse.

She told her son, "I am sorry to say this to you, Thomas, but during your marriage, you've already aged double time because of your high stress, Luella's long wish list, and her continuous mistakes in child raising. Your health is not a joke. Also, she should respect me when I do good things for her and for all of you.

"It is time for you to learn to wisely say 'no' to her wishes and change her parenting style also. You do not have to be the victim of her failing child training. Do not forget, the two boys are your children also; they are not only her property."

No Christmas was pleasing for Thomas's mother with Luella. She always found a way to make Carol feel uncomfortable. She gave the presents out to Rolland before his grandmother's arrival, and most of the time, she made faces like she was too tired to celebrate, especially during Carol's visits.

Luella did not recognize or did not want to recognize at any time her own negative body language toward Carol. Body language speaks volumes about our feelings—more than speaking words. Our body speaks for itself without saying anything, and that takes care of about 80 percent of our communication. Body language involves everything from appearance to facial expression, tone of voice to gestures, and behavior everything. Scientists have found two hundred fifty thousand facial expressions, which can vary from culture to culture.

They cannot be that much different, though. At Christmas a daughter-in-law who is not pleasant and does not have a warm facial expression toward her husband's mother cannot fake a pleasant attitude.

Last Christmas, Luella told Carol that Thomas was going to have a vasectomy so as not to have any more children.

That was very sad news for Thomas's mom because her son already had some health issues. Now, Luella also wanted to control his manhood in addition to his time and money. She wanted to change his bodily function without considering the consequences.

This was for sure not great holiday news for Carol, who went home to cry. After she had cooked for them and given them a lot of gifts for the holidays, she expected a little more love—at least, some kindness.

Her five-year-old grandson had told her, "Grandmother, I am not going to have children because I do not want a heart attack or stroke."

Luckily Carol could hold back her tears at their home because of her grandson's funny comment, but she felt as if someone had put a knife in her heart.

Thomas recognized that his mom left too soon and called her to ask if she was not feeling well.

Carol told him what Luella had said while he was upstairs to bring down toys for the children. She said, "I can see that she does not like me after all that has happened, and that is not surprising because I am not so crazy about her manner either.

"Christmas is the best time of the year, when people celebrate benevolence and love, so it would be more tactful not to mention this kind of topic. Obviously, Luella does not care for my feelings. If your grandma would hear her speech, she would turn in her grave."

Then Carol started to cry hopelessly in her pain. She said, "Why can we not have at least a good Christmas celebration?"

Thomas came over with flowers and apologized for Luella's behavior. He said, "Mom, I did not decide yet. Please don't cry; I will not have this surgery."

Then he turned the situation into a joke and said, "My wife did not know that you opposed this surgery. How about this idea? I will have surgery on myself only if we have a third child. I cannot take any more stress given my already very stressful job and two sons."

Situations like these made Carol sad over her son's marriage and Luella's lack of appreciation for him, which did not help her heart condition.

Luella's narcissistic personality did not let her consider other people's feelings or interests at all. The main thing was that she got everything she wanted, and she was too haughty to admit her own mistakes.

One of their friends told Carol, "She's got your son by his balls, and you cannot do anything. Believe me, if they taught people exploitation in schools, Luella could write a great book about it. She knows all the tricks and also all the lies that can be used to fool others and get everything from them. Often lies are the best talent for some people to build their future."

Carol answered, "I do not want to be malicious, but that is how it looks. I am sad because Thomas is my only child, and I sacrificed my life for his happiness."

Luella told her mother-in-law that her girlfriend was stupid because she asked her boyfriend too soon to buy her things; instead, she should have seduced and tamed him first. "Of course the boyfriend left her," she said.

She knew all of these things too well, but she did not know the future because that was not in her crystal ball. More often than not, she ignored Thomas's opinions and feelings.

Then some unexpected things happened. Rolland was at Grandma's home and watching "Winnie the Pooh." When the cat ran out from her grandson's side, he started to cry.

Carole asked Rolland, "What happened?"

Rolland answered, "I do not know."

Grandma Carol asked her grandson, "How is your karate training going?"

Rolland had administered a punch under Carol's eye to show his expertise. Carol had a black eye for a few days. Now she asked, "Did you not learn the basic rule yet that you are not to attack anybody unless they attack you? Did you do the same to my cat?"

Rolland admitted it and apologized.

Carol realized then that it was time for her to make some changes because things like that and different views on child raising caused stressful situations with Luella that could lead to bad consequences.

She visited a psychic to know what to expect from her future life regarding Luella's behavior and her grandson's manner. Carol did not believe in mystics; she just wanted to hear another somewhat expert opinion.

She told the fortune-teller about Luella's last comment regarding her son's sterilization among other things, and this is what the fortune-teller said: "In my daily practice I meet with grandmothers who are isolated from their children permanently because of in-laws. Let them live their lives and commit their mistakes and be independent. If they need you, they will look for you. Also, ask them to find another babysitter because you do not have to take extra aggravation for anybody. Let your son realize that he is too permissive with his wife, and help them only if they ask you to do so.

"Anyway, there are things in life we cannot change, so then we pray. Remember the old adage that will prevail: 'What has to happen will happen. What has to be done will be done.'

"Believe me, less knowledge often makes happier people. What we do not know in our lives does not give us pain."

Grandmother Carol told Thomas to look for another babysitter, and she went back to work to avoid further heartaches and arguments with her son and his wife.

After seven years of nerve-racking marriage and stressful days, luck hit Thomas like lightning. It came as a surprise for everybody.

A new nurse got hired in the hospital to work at Thomas's side. Her name was Anna, she was born in California, and she looked like a morning star. She was brunette, divorced, kind, and jolly. She had one child, and she admired Thomas very much.

She had worked with Thomas for about six months when her son needed to have his tonsils removed. That was the occasion that Thomas visited his young patient at home.

Anna confessed her love for the doctor and gave him time to think it over. She said, "You have a special place in my heart, Thomas, for your kindness and great personality." They shared a kiss, which sealed the relationship. The attraction was already too deep to be ignored by Thomas, especially after his disappointing marriage with Luella, who very rarely considered his side during their relationship.

Still, Thomas would not divorce because he loved Luella and his two sons very much, but he learned just in time that Luella had had a relationship for several years with her manager. That was too much for Thomas to take.

They separated for a while, but Thomas was not happy because he missed Luella and his sons. Thomas visited his sons twice every week.

His older son, Rolland, told him, "Papa, come back, please, because we miss you too much already and love you. My little brother is crying after you too."

Thomas wanted to return home, but Luella rejected this idea. Shortly after this episode, they divorced, and Thomas left everything for Luella. He did not care about the house and other things; he asked only for the children's custody, but Luella disagreed.

Thomas was heartbroken and said, "Comfort and money are what she wanted in the first place, not love. She loves herself and herself only. Everybody else comes after that. It seems that most of the time, she needed me only as a provider."

Everything comes to an end, because life is about changes, except true love, which makes our life easier and nicer. It shines at holidays and stays with us forever.

The icing on the cake now was that Luella started to be interested in Carol's opinion about their life. That was too late after so many disappointments Luella had caused her. Carol tried her best to help with the grandchildren, but Luella did not really appreciate her help. She never called Carol to ask how she was doing or if she needed anything. She called once a year to wish her a happy birthday, probably at Thomas's request.

The marriage with Thomas was over. Their family life was never harmonious anyway because of Luella's stubborn and selfish behavior.

Carol thought, *God knows his ways. Thomas was already too depressed about his life, although he never complained nor mentioned his many health issues.*

Mothers read from the signs around their children.

Carol told her girlfriend, "I can die easier now that I know my son has somebody who really loves him for himself and not for other advantages. Luella did not deserve Thomas's love, and what we gain undeservedly in our life, we can never really appreciate."

Carol was sad because of her grandchildren's future life. At the same time, she was optimistic that her son had finally found a woman who appreciated and loved him for his qualities. Carol struggled through her whole life for her son's happiness by raising him alone. She sacrificed everything she could for his future. She felt heartbroken about Thomas's unhappy marriage.

Some of these things connect like dots in a puzzle in our lives, but narcissistic personalities usually do not recognize the consequences because they are too busy with their own selves and are blinded by their own greatness. Luella could have made positive changes in their relationship earlier, but she was too busy with her own interests.

She had many good qualities, but she did not use them enough for other people's benefit. She often acted haughty, selfish, and unconcerned.

Fairy tales come true only if we think right and we give true love to other people.

Benevolence toward other individuals makes our lives better and gives purpose to our days. We were not made for our own selves. We can be happy only if we serve others and try our best to be good always to make other people happy around us.

Love and kindness are more important in human relationships than money and advantages.

Luella will learn more about these things through her future experiences and might understand Thomas with his new choice of love. It is sad that she did not learn enough during her relationship with him because she could have saved her marriage. Instead, she went too often overboard with her wishes and haughty manner, when she should have cared more about her husband's feelings and her family connections with Carol, among other things.

The best and most we can have from life is love, and we should treasure it when we find it.

CHAPTER 12

MY START WITH JOAN

In my old country, Hungary, it is sometimes said that "Whoever changes his country, he should also be prepared to change his heart as well." I do not agree. However, any new immigrant should, of course, be open to new experiences and be adaptable to new expectations. He or she should also work to be included in his or her new society.

In the beginning, we as new "explorers" do not always see how some new customs or new information will be meaningful or helpful to us later on. Sometimes we only start to connect the dots in a later phase of our life. This was certainly the case with me and with my friend Joan.

In this country, my favorite job was as a maid, cleaning houses with Joan. It was not the job itself that I enjoyed. Rather, it was Joan's company as we cleaned houses together that I most enjoyed and appreciated. This was now many decades ago.

Joan was in her sixties, when my friends introduced me to her. She was blond, with nice blue eyes. She looked like a guardian angel, and for me, that was who she really was. She was my instructor and my best friend later on.

She gave up her customer service representative job at the Walmart because she had found it to be too high stress. Instead, she established her housecleaning business on her own. She not only cleaned houses, but also helped families with children, such as doing grocery shopping and the like.

Each time we cleaned a house for a family, she left little gifts for the children at the entrance of the house. Everybody liked her.

She also helped me practice my English-speaking skills. She talked to me more slowly so that I could more easily understand her. She wrote down for me some words to study. She also recommended that I take English as a Second Language classes.

At the time, my language skills were between nowhere and zero, but slowly they got better week by week. Sometimes some people even started to understand me. I also learned a lot from Joan about people's habits and basic American customs.

"When people ask you, 'How are you?' they do not expect you to go into details. This is only a greeting," she explained.

Each workday she picked me up with her old Cadillac from our apartment at the time. Then we would together go to large homes to clean them. Usually, we did three houses per day. It took us about six or seven hours. I would clean the kitchen and vacuum. Joan did all the rest. Everything was nice and smelled fresh when we left.

When we were finished at each house, Joan always put a few flowers into a vase. Joan explained to me about the style and design of the houses and of the furniture. While we cleaned houses, I saw a lot of beautifully designed and generally clean homes, but I also saw a lot of messy homes.

"The best way to see the true nature of the people who live in a house," Joan explained, "is to view their kitchen and restrooms. If these places are a mess, you know that you have to watch out with them."

What really surprised me the most was that Joan always gave me exactly half of the home owner's payment for our work.

"Why do you not deduct for the cost of your gasoline and also for your business expenses from me?" I would ask her.

"You just started, and you need help," she said to me, "God knows me, and he gives it back to me in other ways."

I was very thankful to her and loved her as my instructor and my protector.

After our work, we went to eat at a nearby McDonald's. My favorite sandwich was the Big Mac. One time, a young fellow asked me for a date.

"Leave her alone," Joan told the man. "She is a lady and definitely not for you!"

I felt safe and happy with Joan all the time. It was a very big help for me to have her. She also appreciated that I was listening to her and helping her.

On her birthday, I invited her to our place. I cooked a Hungarian dinner for her.

"The last time I ate something this tasty was when my mom still cooked for me," she told me.

I was happy that I could do something for her. She also brought a toy for my son and beautiful flowers for me. I gave her flowers and a watch. It was a very heartwarming day to celebrate her birthday with her. She had raised her two sons alone because her husband had died of cancer when the sons were young.

After three months of cleaning houses with her, I started to go to a dealer school, where I learned how to deal card games, roulette, and craps in a casino. Soon I realized that craps was the least favorite of mine because it was the most hectic and loudest game in the casino. The card games were more fun, but I remembered that back at home, they called cards the "Devil's Bible."

I decided to call my mom by telephone about this.

"If that is your work, it is okay," she told me, "but do not get into the habit of gambling at all. There is a good reason that they call it the 'Devil's Bible.'"

Joan told me the same thing. She also prepared me for the ruthlessness of the casino business.

"It will be tough for you to stand for eight hours and put up with all the drunk and rude customers' comments with a smile," she said.

She was right. The hardest part of a casino dealer's job is to stand erect next to a gambling table for eight hours with a big smile.

Joan also took me to driving school and brought me home. She also took me to the driving test so that once I passed, I would be able to buy a car and drive myself.

"You should always drive in the middle lane," she told me, "where you have more opportunities to navigate if and when somebody else next to you does something silly."

I do not think that I could have succeeded with my new life in this country if Joan had not helped me. May God bless her soul; she was one of the best human beings I have ever known.

After four months of dealer school, I went to my first audition in a downtown casino for a job. I was overly excited. When an ace was on the top, I asked for insurance, but then I recognized that I did not have the requisite bottom card in hand, as I should. However, the auditioning supervisor was nice and smiled. In the end, he hired me because he saw that the way I dealt was accurate and clean.

"You did all right," he said. "You made that one mistake just because of your excitement."

I started first as a dealer on extra board. This meant that I did not have a regular schedule; I was only called into the casino occasionally each week for work. Nevertheless, I was happy to have the job. On my days off, I still went to clean houses with Joan.

"You did okay," she said, "and I think you should rest on your days off. I will do fewer houses from now on."

I almost cried because I did not feel good to say good-bye to my work partner, but I desperately needed the casino's benefits, especially the health insurance coverage.

After I was hired full-time in the casino, our life changed. We moved to a new apartment. My friend Joan came with me to advise me when I needed to buy a used car. My son also was touched by Joan's kindness.

"We are very lucky with Joan," my son said, "because she is treating us as if we were her relatives."

"Yes," I said, "she is my guardian angel for sure."

Two weeks later, I received news that Joan was hit by a car and died. I could not believe it. I was very sad for months due to her tragic loss and went to her grave to pray for her.

Joan's kindness and love still escort me all these years later and through all my struggles. Her company was like a warm blanket that would keep me sheltered in cold and sad days. Just thinking about her words and mannerisms filled me with hope and courage. She helped me so much to adapt to my new country.

"Do not worry," she used to say. "Even though life changes all the time, there will always be new things that can make us happy. Please remember that it does not matter where we come from; it only matters where we are headed."

No matter what happens, we all try to believe that there will be a silver lining, but it is hard to see it when we lose someone who is so near to our heart.

CHAPTER 13

WHAT HAPPENS IN VEGAS WILL NOT STAY IN VEGAS!

I am very fortunate to live in a beautiful place like Las Vegas and to have many good friends and a good job that pays my bills. Indeed, the city provides a lot of fun for everyone. Fun activities are not just limited to gambling alone. There are also world-class shopping, dining, and entertainment options here, along with beautiful suburbs and phenomenal outdoor recreational opportunities. No wonder this is a popular place to live and work.

Although I am fortunate to have a job that pays well and have good friends, I often feel dissatisfied with my actual work as a blackjack dealer. It is a mentally and physically taxing job, which also sometimes involves personal humiliation.

When I look back at my decades-long career as a casino dealer, I still cannot make up my mind whether I like or hate my work. No doubt, in some ways I find my work entertaining.

Each day at work, I meet with people from all walks of life, who are eager to share with me, or all of us at the card table, their respective life stories. I've found that often these stories are interesting or informative. In addition to funny anecdotes, some of the guests provide us with gifts, as appreciation for the good time that they had playing at our table.

On the other hand, to be a dealer also means that I need to adjust myself to the needs of at least fifty strangers per day, as well as to the needs of another fifty employees with whom I work. Such constant adaptation each and every day to new and unpredictable stressful situations can be very difficult and, in some cases, irritating and nearly impossible.

In particular, many of our patrons can be quite intolerant when they are drinking and losing their money. These types of guests often end up going overboard at our expense. Especially when they are losing more than they can afford, they are constantly cursing and calling us by all kinds of names, which are not fit to print at length.

Following one especially difficult day at work, I called my mom.

"I am thankful for my job and for the money," I told her, "because what I make here in one job required me to work three jobs back home in Budapest. I just wish it would be less irritating."

"Do you think it was easier to be an attorney?" my mom responded.

"I will survive as a casino dealer for sure, but some days, I am depressed," I told her. "What I do not like about my job is the guilty feeling that comes with it, because I work for a casino where I am part of a system that takes people's money. I am also under the microscope at all times—constantly being watched and criticized by my supervisors, by our guests, and by coworkers for everything I do. Under this high level of constant scrutiny, it is very hard to feel comfortable in my own skin."

"Try not to take everything too seriously," my mom counseled me. "People are moody, and by the next day, they often forget everything they have said the day before or will have other ideas. Please also get a good rest whenever you can."

"Thank you, Mom, for your advice, but when I am in the moment, it is not always easy to overlook hurtful situations."

"I am sure that you would be better appreciated at home in Hungary with your diploma," my mom responded. "But of course, you would be working for less money."

"It is not just about money," I told her. "As you know, there were several other issues that bothered me in Hungary as well."

Over the decades, I've worked at several casinos. At each casino, I had the misfortune to deal cards to patrons who tried to give me a hard time for just about everything—my look, my performance, and especially my Hungarian accent. I could hardly believe that discrimination could cause so much emotional pain until I experienced it almost daily myself.

"I am sorry for my accent, but I am from a different village, Budapest, just like Zsa Zsa Gabor," I would sometimes say. "She sang in the old television show *Green Acres*. In my version, the song goes like this: 'Green Acres is the place to be. Dealer livin' is the life for me ...'"

Having heard my revised song, one of my coworkers, Joe, along with some others, started to call me Zsazsa. The nickname then stuck. For a long time now, people have called me Zsazsa in the casino.

Some of our patrons had a good laugh once they heard my revised Green Acres song. Sadly, not all the patrons liked my accent, even though there are a myriad of accents in the United States, and even native-born speakers speak with a dialect depending on their region of the country.

"I am not going to play with a fucking foreigner!" one of the patrons said to me after I changed his cash for gaming chips upon his request and wished him "good luck" at my table as he sat down to start playing. He then continued, "Go get the hell out of here! Don't you see that nobody wants you here?"

Thankfully, I was able to take a quick break shortly thereafter. On my way to the break room, I walked by my pit manager, whom I liked very much.

"Why are you crying? Is something wrong?" he asked me.

So I told him what had just happened.

"You should have told this 'pig,'" he responded, "to go home and learn better manners before he steps another foot in our casino!"

Hearing my manager's words, my tears were quickly gone, and I started to laugh. However, my manager's empathy with my plight was unusual. Normally in casinos, supervisors keep repeating the mantra that "the guest is always right!" This means that we have to treat the guest as being correct regardless of what the guest might actually be saying. As dealers, we may never argue with our patrons about anything, provided that the patrons have to observe the casino's rules for the games themselves.

I probably should not take the discriminating guest's words to heart, because about half of the dealers are also immigrants. A large number of our patrons are also either tourists from other countries or other immigrants living in America. I liked our diversity. All of them could share some stories about their own countries, cultures, and experiences. On most days, being surrounded by a throng of foreign tourists and foreign coworkers, I felt comfortable. I did not feel that I belonged to some minority group.

Unfortunately, our jobs required that we separate patrons from their money. This made it feel like a negative job, especially without some headache medication within easy reach. When the players got drunk or they lost, which often happened, they would raise hell. They would call us all kinds of names, ranging from "dragon" and "snake" to "fucking bitch" and the like.

One day, to my surprise, a young man called me "darling." He then asked me to also call him "darling." Then when I finally did call him "darling," he tipped me five dollars.

"My hair stands up on my back from your sexy accent," he said with a big grin. "It is hard for me to think about cards right now."

Luckily, not everybody hated foreigners. Additionally, the dealers would show each other empathy and support whenever one of our patrons went overboard.

One day at work I was assigned to the crazy-four poker game. My red hair was freshly curled, because I just came from the beauty salon. After I greeted the patrons at my table with a bright smile, I began to deal cards. It just happened that my first hand consisted of a three of a kind from the card shuffling machine at my table. However, the patron sitting at the first base position at my table had two pairs, which was a weaker hand.

"Do you see it?" the disappointed patron said to everyone at my table. "The *red rattlesnake* just arrived. Our lucky streak is over. We cannot win a hand anymore!"

It was true that the color of my hair was reddish brown, but it was nicely arranged and, for sure, I did not look like a rattlesnake. However, I could not argue with the player. I had to think of something else.

"I pray every night that I may have *nice players* at my table," I responded to him. "Now, look at me; how fortunate I am that I got them."

When the supervisor, standing close to my table, heard my response, he needed to walk away because he was cracking up laughing. Others were also making jokes. The ill-mannered patron then left the table, but I did not miss him and his comments.

Following this episode, one of the other patrons, who had witnessed these events, returned to my table with his wife. They wanted to take a picture with me.

"We had the time of our life at your table," the wife said to me. "This was a time filled with laughter, even though we lost."

I was happy to hear that they enjoyed my service and company, especially after I was called a "rattlesnake" by the other guest. The kind couple's compliment was a nice break from the torrent of insults many of our patrons usually hurl at us. Sadly, potty mouth is a common occurrence in Las Vegas casinos, especially for those patrons who are under the influence of alcohol and lose their money.

Undoubtedly, to increase personal growth, some criticism, including self-criticism, can be healthy. However, to listen to a constant stream of harsh and critical comments from our guests each day without the ability to respond can make anyone paranoid. It can certainly create an unhealthy sense of guilt. I was almost there.

Even without harsh criticism, the atmosphere is filled with constant pressure to perform. "Give me the king of diamonds!" or "Give me the queen of hearts!" and so on are the words we hear constantly from our patrons. To be honest, such prodding can irritate the hell out of any dealer, because card dealers do not have the ability to determine the sequence of cards whatsoever.

I remember that one evening at work, one of the patrons stood up and blew his cigar smoke straight into my face.

"I will stop when you give me a blackjack!"

"I am only a dealer, not a magician," I told him. Then I politely smiled without saying anything else. Luckily, the next hand that I was able to deal him was a blackjack.

"Please remember your promise," I told him.

But he did not stop and kept blowing his cigar smoke straight into my face.

"Now you have to give me another twenty-one," he said.

I called the table-game supervisor over to my table. He told the player to leave.

"Our dealers are not here so that you can abuse them," the supervisor explained.

Sadly, these situations get even worse when some of the patrons start banging on the game table or start slapping the dealer's hand or throw their drink on the table intentionally. I've experienced it all.

I had a customer who played $300 to $500 per hand on blackjack. Each time he lost, he would hit the table hard with his fist a couple of times and then jump up and down on his chair like an enraged simian in a cage. Each time that he did this, the table was shaking so hard that even the rack on my side of the table, where we keep the casino's money, was moving up and down. I was shaking as well.

After three hours of such aggressive behavior being on display, I became especially concerned. I feared that if this patron were to lose significantly more, he might try to hit me as well. Just a few days earlier, one of the other casino dealers, a young girl who was working with me on the same shift, was physically assaulted by one such patron. I was scared that my patron would do the same to me.

On the next hand that I dealt, we both had cards that totaled nineteen. This meant that it was a "push"—neither I nor the patron had won the hand.

"Push!" I said, as my training required.

When he heard me, he was grinding his teeth. Then he hit the table with his fist even harder this time. A really loud bang could be heard. A few of his chips even rolled away.

"I am so sorry, sir," I said as I looked up after removing the cards from the table. "Our casino does not let me pay for bets where the house and the player have the same face value, no matter how hard you hit the table."

"Do not say anything to him because he is a highly valued customer," whispered in my ear the floor supervisor, who rushed over when he heard the thumping noise coming from my table.

"All right," I whispered back to my supervisor in response. *This guy only needs a straitjacket and a cage, and he would be welcome at the zoo anytime,* I thought to myself.

Following the completion of my shift at work, I would usually walk out from the casino to the employee parking lot with my friend Mary. One time, she told me that some patrons were picking on her for not smiling. Then when she did smile, another patron said, "We know why you smile—you are happy to take our money!"

"It seems," Mary said to me. "that we are never good enough for them, no matter how hard we try to do our best! They make us feel that we are only as good as the last hand that we dealt …"

"I agree," I replied to Mary. "We should be vaccinated against some of these rude customers. After all the hard times I've had to endure from players, even plastic surgery could not fix my face again to make me look normal."

"I do not see anything wrong with your face," Mary responded. "I think that is only your imagination that makes you think that. Maybe Hollywood is going to call you tomorrow to offer you a job."

We then had a good laugh as we were reaching the employee parking lot.

"Free at last. Free at last. Thank God Almighty, we are free at last!" we both said as we were getting closer to our cars, getting ready to drive away from work.

We then both had another good laugh about our daily misery at the casino, which helped to relieve some of that day's stress and paranoia.

"I will pray to God for forgiveness for my *thoughts*—those wishes of misfortune that I made as to some of our worst customers," I told her.

Given the high pressure of our job, we always tried to maintain a healthy balance with plenty of laughter. Laughter is not only the shortest distance between two people; it is the best cure for any irritating situation. Additionally, often after work, our bodies desperately needed a good pressure point massage, especially in our necks and backs. A good massage at an affordable salon made for good maintenance of our health.

Sadly, casinos are often run like military bases, with requirements for their casino dealers such as (1) shut up and deal; (2) if you say anything, keep it short; (3) do not ask for any favors, even if you are ill; (4) when customers are rude, first pretend that you did not hear them; (5) do not argue, no matter how many insults are hurled at you; (6) keep smiling no matter what, even if the patron curses at you; and (7) many other similarly oppressive requirements.

With my friend Mary, who had worked with me for about fifteen years as a casino dealer, we always found a way to uplift our spirits; we made jokes about almost everything.

One ordinary day, a man walked by my gaming table and asked for directions to the bathroom. Once I told him how to get there, he then said to me, "Can you also put your finger up my ass?"

I was shocked. The man was good-looking and well dressed. On the surface, he looked like a gentleman. Before he opened his mouth, I would even have considered him for a date. His insulting words, however, had completely destroyed that positive first impression. I could only gasp for air.

"Sir, you have, you have such wonderful manners." I told him once I regained my composure. "Next time, please, do not practice your manners on me."

Fortunately, he quickly left. A little later, I told Mary what had happened. She was quick to counsel me.

"You were too polite," Mary told me. "You should have said: 'not my finger but my foot, if you do not speed along quickly.'"

Later that evening, I went on break from my table. I could see that some of my dealer coworkers were surreptitiously showing each other their index fingers, jabbing upward, with a knowing smile on their faces. I knew that they were having fun at my expense, because they had all heard about the restroom customer from Mary. I was not amused that they all knew what had happened; however, I'd forgotten to tell Mary to keep the story a secret.

The following day at work, we had just returned from our break when our elderly floor person was waiting for us in our section of the gaming tables. Many of us knew that he'd previously served in the military, and he could be very brief and concise.

"Mary; Lee," he said. Then he looked at us with urgent anticipation that his orders would be followed.

Surprised and confused, Mary looked at me.

"Who is Mary Lee?" she asked me.

"What he meant was, 'Mary, please switch with Lee at his table, so that Lee can now go on his next break." I translated the old floor person's words to Mary. Everybody who knew the old floor person was laughing about Mary's misunderstanding.

In most cases, table assignment was fairly rigid—a dealer was assigned to certain games for his or her entire shift. Under this system, a casino dealer might sometimes deal from the same table for weeks. At other times, casinos used the rubber band system to assign dealers. A rubber band system is a system of randomly assigning dealers who are not otherwise assigned to a specific table during a shift. The system is called a rubber band system as a rubber band is often placed around the clipboard under the name of the last dealer assigned in this manner.

All of this would be at the complete discretion of the pit managers. In most cases, casino pit managers use the rubber band system only at the end of the work shift, when they start closing down tables. At this time, it makes more sense to rotate dealers. Earlier in the workday, however, it would normally be too time-consuming to randomly assign dealers each time one went on a break.

In one of the old casinos in downtown Las Vegas, where I first worked as a table-game dealer, management assigned me for months to the very same blackjack table that had a malfunctioning air-conditioning unit directly above it. Given this malfunction, it was freezing cold at this table at all times. I felt as if ice water was being poured down on my head for eight hours each day. The table also had the lowest limit, which attracted the loudest and least refined members of our patronage. Nobody wanted to work there. It was pure torture.

Following two months of hard work under these terrible conditions, I became very ill. My head, my throat, my ears, and even my teeth were in constant pain. I was on medication.

I politely asked the assistant pit manager to send me to another table. She told me to bring a doctor's note first, as it was apparently required for any such table-game reassignment. So the next day,

I returned to work with the doctor's note, and I gave it to the pit manager himself. However, he became very angry.

"I could have done this for you earlier, out of friendship, without a doctor's note," he told me. "But now that you have brought this note, I will need you to bring another doctor's note so that I might be able to make the change. Your new doctor's note should also tell me how long you have to stay away from the cold, and then, I might be able to work out some reassignment to another table. For now, you need to keep working at your assigned table."

"Sorry," I told my manager. "Your assistant pit manager advised me to bring this note, as this is what was required for at least the near term. Unfortunately, he is not here today."

Sadly, another week went by without a change. I could not stand being treated like this.

"Instead of taking him so seriously, you should just seduce him," one of my coworkers who had heard about my problems advised me. "He likes to go out with female employees, sometimes more than one, and have orgies with them. He may have given you a hard time as a way to get you."

I went home and cried half the night. The following day, I lodged a complaint with the director of the casino operation for the harassing ill treatment that I received from the pit manager. I was already under a lot of stress because I was raising my son alone. I did not want to lose my job. I never even called in sick. I do not know how I had the courage to stand up for myself.

"It would be better for you to learn quickly that, here, it does not matter to anyone if you are right or wrong," my pit manager told me once he found out about my complaint. Then he picked up a soup cup in front of him to demonstrate his point. "This spoon will never dip into this soup if I do not want it. You are like the spoon. You need to remember that in the casinos, your boss is always right."

He, of course, meant that he had all the power in the casino and I could go fly a kite with my rights. The only positive outcome from this entire incident was that our casino finally fixed the air-conditioning unit over my worktable.

Following five more difficult years of maltreatment at this casino, especially by this particular pit manager, I was able to find a better job. I quit. On my last day, my unjust pit manager decided to engage me in a conversation yet again.

"Regardless of where you go, I think that you are going to be all right," he said.

I never expected such a comment from him on my last day. However, at that moment, I forgave him for his earlier ill treatment.

At my next employer, I got very lucky. It was one of the happier Las Vegas Strip casinos, where I made more money and got better treatment, at least for a while. Then we went through several changes in management. The owner of the hotel casino also changed. Then one day, we were told that we would have a new manager yet again—Miss Lynn. Most of my coworkers strongly disliked Miss Lynn for good reason.

She made up brand-new rules for us to follow. She then purchased for each game table a dealing shoe that was capable of holding eight decks of cards. Since dealing shoes hold multiple decks of playing cards, they allow for more games to be played by reducing the time between shuffles, and there is less chance of dealer cheating. In some games, such as blackjack, where card counting is a possibility, using multiple decks of cards can also increase the casino's advantage.

Sadly, we were not fortunate with her acquisition of the particular dealing shoes that she had purchased. She bought the cheapest quality model, which she likely got from the lowest bidder.

When we were dealing cards from her new shoes, no dealer could get their cards out from the shoe without an extra push. At the same time, the cover plate of the shoe was quickly damaged or broken, resulting in sharp edges around the dispensing area of the shoe. As a result, several table-game dealers cut and injured their hands by the sharp edges of the broken shoes. Some of the dealers even had their cuts becoming infected, as they were reinjured by these shoes repeatedly.

Yet instead of buying quality equipment to replace the defective and dangerous dealing shoes she had bought in the first place, Miss Lynn started to measure all of the dealers' hand speeds to make sure that we were moving fast enough. If we were deemed slow, she would threaten us with termination.

How many hands a dealer is able to deal in one hour depends on many factors. Miss Lynn's requirement was that we deal four hundred cards per hour. Miss Lynn was critical of everybody, but even more so if the dealer was born in a different country.

She told one of my coworkers, a girl from Thailand, that she needed to cut short her long hair because it was not good for the business. Yet my coworker's hair was beautiful. At work, she even nicely put it up with hair clips. Still it was not good enough for Miss Lynn. My coworker was in tears after Miss Lynn admonished her about cutting her hair short.

During this time, Miss Lynn regularly scheduled me to work twelve days in a row, even though I was already a permanent employee with an assigned five-day-a-week work schedule. On my twelfth day at work, she then assigned me to the Let It Ride poker game, which we dealers, among ourselves, called the Let Me Die poker game. This new name for the game came about because the game required even more intense concentration than blackjack, and when winning hands were not forthcoming, the players whose favorite this game was would complain loudly and endlessly.

One of the players at my table was sitting with his apparent girlfriend and was betting $100 each hand. He and his girlfriend kept showing their cards to each other all the time. This was against the casino's rules for the game. After I dealt the player a full house, I paid out to him $3,300 in accordance with his bet.

Then I really needed to remind him of the rules, as I was required to do by my employer.

"I would like to kindly ask you a favor, sir. Please do not show your cards to each other, because it is against the casino's house rules."

Sadly, the patron's reaction was incredibly hideous. After all, he was just the beneficiary of a great winning hand that I had dealt to him.

"You asshole!" he retorted. "I have been a customer here longer than you have been a dealer. I will make sure that they kick you out from this casino. I will play this game the way I want to play it."

Faced with such a situation, I called over the table-game supervisor for help. The table-game supervisor then proceeded to tell him the same thing that I told him about the game's rule. The irate patron then also called my supervisor an asshole.

He then took the big pile of money that he had won at my table and got up without even saying "thank you"—as if he had earned his big winnings. All of this would be fine, but then he tried to make sure that I would lose my job. This was especially ugly.

To my misfortune, Miss Lynn just happened to walk by the player, and so they talked. Later, Miss Lynn called me to her office to discipline me. She told me that I should not talk to this kind of guest at all.

"Understood, and I am sorry that he was unhappy, but nobody told me that before I was assigned to his table. I thought that my job was to make sure that everyone followed the rules. I did not know that I needed to ignore the rules for him," I said.

Even though I was contrite and was merely asking the player to observe the rules, which we are always required to do, Miss Lynn gave me a warning slip.

"You are not nice at all," she told me. "You are a bad dealer."

To add insult to injury, all of this, of course, happened on the twelfth day of work, since she regularly scheduled me for twelve-day workweeks. A warning slip now allowed them to quickly pursue my termination if they chose to do so.

In the end, I lodged a complaint against Miss Lynn, following several other similar episodes of her loving management. At that time, I heard from the director of the casino operations that the casino already had many other complaints against her, and therefore, I should not feel bad for having to bring this to his attention.

"No wonder that she is so extreme," one of the bartenders told me. "She drinks at least two shots of whisky each day."

"Miss Lynn has lots of complaints against her," chimed in someone from security. "She receives death threats daily. We have to escort her out to her car in the parking lot each day."

After several dealers quit and countless others complained, the casino's management finally fired Miss Lynn for her devious and heartless personality. Following this incident, I worked for another ten years at this casino, under good circumstances, before the ownership changed again. During those ten years, I had lots of laughter and good times with customers and coworkers at work. There was a lot of teasing and a lot of good times to be had.

Following one relaxing vacation in Thailand, I was especially smiling from ear to ear. In Thailand, I had a great time. Each day, I would enjoy a massage and good food. It is a beautiful and exotic country, with very friendly natives. When I returned to work, I shared stories about my vacation with my coworkers, including my experience with great massages.

Joe, one of my coworkers, made jokes about my trip and the massages. He said that I came back with a big smile because I found "Ramon." I guess in Joe's mind, Ramon was my ideal hot masseur.

"Ramon, please bring a towel; Miss Zsazsa would like to have another massage," Joe would say to the other dealers whenever he would walk by my table into the pit area, where all the table games were located.

Everyone would have a good laugh. Then the customers at my table became curious.

"Who is this Ramon?" the players at the table would ask me.

"I wish I knew," I would respond. "Joe made him up for me."

Following Joe's friendly teasing, one of the players kept following me throughout the whole night from one game table to the next.

"Zsazsa," he said, "do not forget about me! I will wait for you in room 204. We will have champagne in my hot tub ..."

"Yes, of course!" I replied with a smile. "You will have champagne in your room, and I will have champagne in my room at home. As you can see, I still have a lot of work to do here."

We had good times and bad times, but no matter what, all of us dealers tried our best to do a good job, to be on time, and to protect the casino's interest consistently with the rules.

Joe was a very nice guy. Everybody loved him, because he stayed positive and good-natured. Even Joe, however, became very upset a couple of weeks later when a drunk patron threw a bottle of beer at him.

Following that event, another coworker told me that, in the end, he was not too surprised by this incident involving a misbehaving patron. At his earlier job, one drunk player urinated on a gaming table after the player lost all his money.

"Nobody knew whether that urinating player was expressing his opinion about the game or was just marking his territory," John would later joke about the incident. Apparently when it happened, the player unzipped his pants at the gaming table and started to proceed as if he was next to a urinal. Taken back by all of this, the dealer was shouting to the floor person by his name: "Frank, Frank!" The floor person, however, failed to turn around, as he was on the phone. So he just said, "Oh, go ahead!" The drunk patron with the open zipper apparently misunderstood the situation and "went ahead." Sadly, it took a few more minutes before casino security personnel could grab him and throw him out from the casino, along with the permanently damaged card table.

On the following day, Susan, one of my coworkers, told me that in the middle of her game, the supervisor delivered money to her table. Then, in front of the players, her supervisor said to her, "Close your eyes and open your thighs. Big daddy is home!"

The supervisor was suspended for sexual harassment.

On Labor Day weekend, a group of swindlers came to our casino. There were six of them. They would together occupy a single gaming table. They made up all kinds of strange stories to detract the dealer at their table. At other times, to misdirect the dealer's attention, they would throw their drinks on the table. Most significantly, they were cupping their bets and switching their cards.

Cupping or covering one's bet is not allowed because it provides an opportunity to change one's wager after the outcome of the game is known. On the other hand, by switching cards, the cheater attempts to influence the game outcome itself.

It is one thing to try to get under the dealer's skin. It is another to cheat or destroy property. They did, however, finally arouse the dealer's attention that night.

Unfortunately, the security personnel arrived too late with the handcuffs. The swindlers left before security got there.

The dealer at whose table the swindlers played was questioned. She was asked what she knew about these individuals. She did not know anything, and they disappeared without a trace. They showed the video of the cheaters playing at her table to the dealer. She cried and said, "I felt that something was not right, but I was not sure what it was."

In addition to those who tried to cheat at cards, we also had a wide range of inebriated partyers at the casino. There were, for instance, some young ladies who loved to hold their bachelorette parties in our casino.

"Be nice and give me money, because I have to pay for my school," one of them once told me.

"I hope that I can. We will see how the game goes." I told the future bride. "By the way, I would like to compliment you; you look great and smell great."

"The perfume is Prada," she answered. "And my pussy smells like Prada too!"

"It might be better to keep some things private," I replied.

Working in a casino, we regularly encountered surprises and have seen plenty of unforgettable events. Some of these events were especially stressful.

To be a dealer in a casino is a lot like being a gladiator. It is a constant fight for the casino's interests in the noisy, smoke-filled, overwhelming arena of the casino. Often the "fight" takes the form of mental abuse and, in some cases, even physical abuse by our patrons and by our management. It is painful to carry on daily with our visible and invisible wounds with the required big smile.

We, as casino dealers, always had to protect the casinos' interest, but the casinos did not protect our interest in return. While the casinos are at the top of the field in making money, they are at the bottom of the field in the treatment of their employees, with very few exceptions. The casino industry is too focused on profits and would much rather hush away their workers' problems than solve them. The gaming industry's strict regulations only apply to the business of making money, not to the business of treating employees well.

In any event, I was happy that I was always able to work. I also enjoyed meeting so many nice, kindhearted, and funny individuals through my work. The part that I did not like was those interactions that I was forced to have with some of our shadier patrons and some of our casino managers, who had shockingly callous employment practices.

Unfortunately, I could never call in sick to work, because I was raising my son as a single mother. I wanted to show dependability at my job. I remember that, even when my ankle became badly twisted and swollen, I was still too afraid to call in sick because it was the weekend and the casino needed all their dealers to show up for work. No excuses would be entertained.

Two days later, I was finally able to see a doctor with my ankle.

"It looks really bad," the doctor told me after he saw my ankle. "If you do not rest, this leg may need to be amputated."

Nevertheless, even with all the hardship, I was still reluctant to change to a different career. To hold any job involves stress and some unjust treatment. In my case, stress, disappointments, and the hard work as a casino dealer took their toll on my health and my beliefs. It, of course, matters not only what we do, but also how we are able to do it.

"It is what it is," Mary once told me. "We have to take the good with the bad."

"You are right," I told her. "However, in those situations when you are being treated very unjustly, it is difficult to react with a happy attitude. The best that I can do is to think to myself: 'Forgive them for they do not know what they do.'"

Over the years, there were various happenings at work that occasionally caused great sadness, but my friends and the massages helped me to forget my pain. Surely, whenever we had caring and supportive managers and a good group of friends at work, we experienced better times. In the gaming industry, it is the central tenet of "management by love" that casino dealers are the eyes, the hands, and the front line of the casino business. The way your employees feel is the way your customers will feel. And if your employees do not feel valued, neither will your customers.

Most of our managers understood these things, and they were very supportive. However, there were always some exceptions—some bad apples in the basket.

In addition to the hard work and some disappointments, it was fun to be a table-game dealer. I was included in greater events and life around me, which made me happy most of the time. Our job also made many people's days more enjoyable and fun. That was important for us.

With regard to those negative experiences I had working in casinos, I agree with the character named Sakini in the 1956 movie *The Teahouse of the August Moon*. In the movie, Sakini says, "Pain make man think. Thought make man wise. Wisdom make life endurable."

We can all draw our own conclusions, of course, about the casino industry. In my case, my conclusions were based upon my life and my work experience as a casino dealer. I always appreciated nice people and tried my best to make them happy. When I could make people happy, it made my job worthwhile in itself. Everybody knows casinos are meant for gambling. Nevertheless, I felt that by showing things on my side of the table, I might help some patrons appreciate their dealers' work lives as well.

CHAPTER 14

MY UNFORGETTABLE JOURNEY

I have lived in the United States for three decades. Following many stressful years of adjustment to a new life in a new land and years of hard work, I decided that it was finally time for me to visit my relatives and my old friends in Budapest, Hungary, which is my old country.

Budapest is one of the most beautiful cities in Europe. Viking Cruises, in its television commercial, regularly uses images of the city, including its historical parliament building, to advertise its river cruises. The two halves of the city stretch out on both banks of the Danube River.

Given its separation by the Danube, Budapest, originally, was two cities, named Buda and Pest. The city has a two-thousand-year-old history, with numerous historical buildings, theaters, thermal baths, gourmet restaurants with Gypsy music, and friendly folks. Walking over the Danube on the Chain Bridge from Pest to Buda and looking at the beauty of both sides of the city is pure perfection.

Before I moved away for good, my family and I lived in the suburbs of Budapest, in an area full of large homes with even larger gardens. Each spring, the cherry trees and many other flowers came into beautiful bloom. Walking along the streets, the vision of beautiful gardens would fill one's eyes. Neighbors knew one another by their first names. We enjoyed our lives there, especially our childhood, which was filled with lots of fun.

Sadly, before I was able to return to Budapest, my mother passed away. I found her old house, my childhood home, empty, abandoned, and lonely. Her coffee cup, family photographs, Bible, and reading glasses were still on the living room table as reminders of her daily life. She had fallen asleep, and she never woke up again.

My mother was always kind and compassionate to everyone. She was ready to help out not only her family members, but everyone else as well. All her friends and neighbors respected her for her loving, sweet, and kind personality. Over a hundred and forty people showed up to her funeral, even though my mother was a simple housewife, and only a very small number of personal invitations were sent out.

Sadly, I could not even be there for her funeral. At the time of my mother's death, I did not have in my hand my US passport. Unfortunately, I needed to wait two more months to receive it. At that time, the waiting period for passports was longer. Then I was finally able to go.

During my visit to Budapest, everything in my mother's house was still the same way as my mother had left it the day that she passed. My brother's wife was waiting for me to see everything the way it was. She wanted me to see my mother's house as it was on that fateful day, and so, she did not move anything. My brother and sister-in-law were taking care of my mother in her final years.

"I wanted you to choose some things from your mother's belongings to take home with you to Las Vegas," my sister-in-law said.

I looked around. Then I broke down in tears when I found some of my old personal items in her wardrobe on the top shelf. There I found my old embroidered pillowcase and doilies, which I had made when I was seventeen, all of them still clean and neatly arranged by my mother. There was my white blouse, which my mom had made beautiful for me with her embroidery when I was young.

In her Bible, my mother kept a farewell letter for all of us, her three children. In it, she wrote that "I am very proud of all of you and always loved each of you equally. I hope that you will always love and help one another. God's most important commandment to all of us is to love one another with endless love."

My heart was broken because it was difficult for me to accept that my mother had died without me being able to hug her once again and say good-bye to her. Because of months of unfortunate delay in getting a new passport, I even missed her funeral.

Before my plane landed in Budapest, my closest friends and relatives in Hungary were worried about me, as my flight did not arrive on its scheduled day. When my flight finally did arrive in Budapest, they were all happy to see me and greeted me as if I had only left the day before, even though more than two decades had already passed.

However, because my flight was delayed by more than a day, I could not meet with my friends at the airport. Waiting for me in vain, they had left the airport the day before. Instead, my brother, who lives in Budapest, had to pick me up from the airport, and I was finally able to see some of my old friends that evening at my brother's home and even more of them during the next few days in the city.

"How was your flight?" those of them who were not familiar with the specific circumstances of my delay would often politely ask.

"I will tell you about my flight later," I would usually respond, because in truth, my flight was irritating, scary, and took way too long, but I did not want to get into it. I did not want to start out with such a story of misadventure after so many years of being apart. I was also exhausted and not just because of the time difference. A flight that should have taken one day from Las Vegas to Budapest ended up taking two and a half days.

This was the first time in twenty-four years that I was able to travel to my old country, Hungary. In America, I struggled alone, as a single mother, to raise my son. I wanted to do all that I could to help my son to continue with his studies. Fortunately, he was a very good student and was ultimately admitted into a graduate program in one of the most prestigious universities. I was very proud of him.

At the time of my departure to Budapest, my son took me to the airport in Las Vegas. He gave me two pieces of good advice.

"Please, Mom," he said, "first, do me a favor and try not to get on the wrong airplane, which will fly you to Africa, because I cannot find you there. Second, please try to avoid talking to strangers, especially strange men." He said all of this with a bit of a grin. I did sometimes get into a bit of trouble from being forgetful or not being careful enough.

Giving due consideration to my son's "fatherly advice," I went to the correct departure gate and sat down in my assigned seat on my Delta flight, which was a connecting flight through New York. As in a typical economy class, the seats were very narrow and very close to one another.

My seat was the first seat in a bank of three connected seats. In the next seat, there was a gentleman. In the seat next to him sat a lady, reading a magazine.

We had just reached cruising altitude when the gentleman sitting next to me offered me the contents of his lunch box, which contained crackers, nuts, cheese sticks, and so on.

"Please feel free to choose anything that you would like to try," he said.

I looked at him with a bit of hesitation, and perhaps with a bit of caution and surprise. *Why is this man approaching me like a candyman?* I thought to myself.

"Okay," he added, "you may have my sausage too!"

"Isn't that too soon?" I replied. "My son just advised me not to talk to any strangers and not to take a flight to Africa."

Hearing my words and seeing my expression, the gentleman had a good laugh. He then introduced his wife, the lady seated at his other side. When his wife paid attention and heard her husband tell her about our conversation, she laughed out so loud that the flight attendant came to make sure that we were okay.

So we also told the flight attendant about my son's advice and our conversation about my neighbor's lunch box and sausage. She was laughing out loud. In the end, all the passengers in the entire section of the plane where we were seated were laughing out loud with us.

My son's advice about being careful was based upon earlier life experience. A few weeks prior to my flight, I took a seat accidentally in a wrong car at the gasoline station.

It was late at night after a long day of exhausting work. I was very tired. My friend had given me a ride home in his car.

On the way home, we stopped at a gas station. While my friend filled up his car with gasoline, I walked over to the adjacent convenience store to buy myself breakfast.

When I finished shopping, I walked out of the store to the parking lot that separated the convenience store from the gas station, where my friend was filling up his car with gasoline moments ago. I thought that I saw my friend's beige-colored car parked right at the store's entrance. It certainly looked identical to my friend's car. I quickly opened the door and hopped in.

I finally realized my mistake when a large man was staring at me from the driver's seat. He did not look pleased at all. Luckily, he did not try to kidnap me.

"Sorry; I made a mistake," I said. "It seems that I got into the wrong car."

"I know," he replied. "And you did surprise me."

Undoubtedly, my son remembered this recent incident when he told me not to get on the wrong plane. Indeed, I was very lucky that the stranger did not drive away with me. I could have ended up somewhere in the Mojave Desert.

The other reason that my son keeps counseling me is that I guess he no longer likes getting my motherly advice now that he is all grown up. Once he gave me the movie *Stop! Or My Mom Will Shoot*, with Sylvester Stallone and Estelle Getty, as a reminder that he does not need a diaper anymore.

So now, he'd rather give me advice than take advice from me. We have certainly reversed our respective roles. Sometimes it is as if I were his daughter and not his mom.

It seems that I do more often need his help than he needs mine. Times change, and people do as well. Sometimes such change happens right in front of our eyes, but we do not recognize it for a long time.

In any event, my flight to Budapest was connecting through New York City. When my plane was approaching New York City's airport, the pilot came on the loudspeaker and announced that there was a tornado scare in the entire region, and therefore, we could not land at our intended destination.

We circled for approximately one hour looking for a place to land. We almost ran out of fuel. Finally, our pilot was given permission to make an emergency landing in Philadelphia.

When we landed, I needed to change planes and try to find some connection to New York. As I was looking for a possible connection to put me back on my original route, I heard a man howl behind me.

"Hey, lady, you over there," he said to me. "You took the wrong plane; this one was flying to Africa!"

A few people laughed. I guess they understood that he was only joking. However, at first I was surprised and upset, as I did not recognize him right away nor did I realize that he was just making a joke. Then I understood that this man was one of the other passengers from my earlier flight. I believe that originally he was from St. Petersburg, Russia. He had apparently listened to my conversation with the couple in the seat next to me on the plane about my son's advice.

Four hours later, we were allowed to fly over to Kennedy Airport in New York City, where my flight would have connected to Budapest. However, it was already close to ten o'clock at night. All flights to Europe were already gone.

From then on, my flight to Budapest was no longer a laughing matter. We stood in the airport with hundreds of other people stranded, who were also there because of the tornado watch in the region. Women stood in line to the restroom; children cried. Everybody was irritated by the entire situation.

There were no services available that late, no vacant rooms for rent, not even any open seats left at the airport. All the hotel rooms were occupied in the area close to the airport.

In the end, I placed my coat on one of the windowsills at the airport; I had decided that I would just sit there that night and wait until more flights would become available in the morning. Fortunately, I found myself in the company of a friendly Mormon Irish couple. They were just returning from a visit with friends in the Salt Lake City area. They tried to lift my spirits.

"We can have a breakfast at seven in the morning," they offered. "After breakfast, we should be able to arrange new flights back to Europe."

Just as they finished speaking, I had to jump up from my windowsill seat and scream. What happened was that a horde of mice just ran out between my legs from underneath the windowsill.

As the night wore on, the Kennedy Airport was looking more and more like a homeless shelter. People were spread out on the airport's dirty floor everywhere. Nobody knew for sure when and how they could take their next flight, because all the ticket counters and information posts were closed. No help was available whatsoever until the next morning.

Luckily, the kind Mormon couple let me make a call on their cellular phone so that I could advise my brother in Budapest that my flight had been indefinitely delayed and that I did not know when I would be able to make it. At that time, I made a promise to myself that, in the future, I would never again book a flight that connected in or even flew over Kennedy Airport.

To try to relax, I started to walk around the airport. Yet it was not relaxing at all, as there were too many people spread out on the airport's floor everywhere. A man from India decided to try to start up a conversation with me, because, as he told me, he liked me. However, I was not in the mood for anyone's courtship.

Thanks to the Irish couple, I survived the "horrors" of that night at the airport with a bit less stress. Unfortunately, scheduling a flight to Europe the next morning did not go well either.

At first, my airline gave me a seat on a flight that was departing in just ten minutes. I obviously missed that flight. The next available flight, in which they gave me a seat connected through another European city, presented a further delay.

When I finally arrived in Budapest, my old hometown, after twenty-four years of absence, I was completely exhausted. In the end, it took me two and a half days, without sleep, to get there. Almost every step of the way, my journey was filled with anxiety-producing uncertainties.

Sadly, nobody was waiting for me at the airport in Budapest. I called my brother from the airport on his cellular telephone to tell him that I finally did arrive. He had already given up and was on his way home from the airport when I reached him, with a large bouquet of two-day-old flowers in his car.

I also called other friends and relatives who had already waited for me two days in the row at the airport with no success. Sadly, they all went to the airport twice without meeting with me at least once. No wonder they were all interested about my difficult flight.

For a long time, people have believed that flying by plane is more predictable and secure than driving a car. Following my experience with such travel issues and seeing stories of several airplane crashes in the news, I am not so sure that is the case, and in any event, I am not too keen on traveling much in the future.

I believe that people are not safe anywhere, but even less so on an airplane, because of all the craziness that is going on in this world. In my case, my plane could only arrive two and a half days later because of a series of issues and mishaps. There could also always be reasons for a delay or worse, reasons that are only understood later.

My son's fatherly advice made the first leg of my flight somewhat fun; however, it did not change the fact that, after many years of hoping to make my visit to my old country, I arrived in tears and abandoned. As I stepped off the plane, nobody was there waiting for me.

Following a few days of recovery in my brother's home in Budapest, I was happy to meet with my relatives and friends again after having been apart for so many years. Their loving care quickly restored me. They treated me as a special guest. All of them treated me as if I left Hungary only the day before.

Everyone kept feeding me everywhere I went. We had daily celebration dinners, consisting of all kinds of delicacies from grilled goose to strudel. Indeed, I ended up gaining ten pounds in just a short time. When I stepped on a weight scale upon my return to Las Vegas, I was happy to be back home in the United States because it seemed that my return home from Budapest had surely saved me from morbid obesity.

It was so nice to visit my old country, to meet with my relatives and with childhood friends, and to feel their love. It was very heartwarming to feel the love of all the people there from my old life. It was also fun to eat in beautiful restaurants with Gypsy music, where the violinist would play Enrico Toselli's "Nightingale Serenade" while all the delicacies were being served. It was beautiful to see the historical bridges over the Danube, with their nighttime lights. In the end, my journey to my old country was very refreshing and fun.

When I finally returned home to Las Vegas, I realized that half of my clothing in my closet did not fit me anymore. Such a realization was not a happy moment for me.

I picked up my telephone to call my mom in Budapest and tell her that they had a bit overfed me. While I was thankful for their love, I was unhappy with all the extra pounds I had packed on.

Then, suddenly, I realized. *What am I doing? Where my mother has gone, there is no phone anymore,* I told myself.

This was a very sad reality, which made me cry and cry again.

I guess you can take someone out of her country, but you cannot take out the memories of her country from her heart. The memories of one's mother and of one's motherland will always live in one's heart.

It is often great fun and refreshing to travel to new countries and to learn about new cultures. It is also great to live in freedom in the United States, with all the conveniences that this country offers. My son and I both have many new friends and deep roots here. Yet, good or bad, we always will worry about all our relatives, friends, and the people we love, no matter where they may live on this earth, because they all remain part of our lives.

CHAPTER 15

BACK TO THE FUTURE IN HUNGARY

No matter where we live, our survival requires a lot of struggles and fights. Throughout humankind's history, it was always like this. Our destinies are, to a considerable extent, also beyond our control and often subject to the greater events of history.

Thus, we live with constant change. At a later time in our lives, we are sometimes faced with our earlier selves. This may surprise us or even comes with some painful realizations.

It was a hot summer night in Budapest, Hungary. My two brothers, Steven and Andy, and I spread out on big comfortable chairs on the patio of Steve's beautiful house, which also has a large welcoming garden. We were enjoying the perfumed garden air and Royal Tokaji wine and had just ordered some fresh pizza. We were waiting for the imminent arrival of our childhood friend Attila.

At that time, Andy and I already had lived in America for several decades. However, we both enjoyed spending time with our brother, Steven, who had remained in Hungary, notwithstanding our departures.

"I never thought that I would end up living in America," I told my brothers. "I certainly did not think that I would live in Las Vegas. Thirty years ago, I would have laughed if someone had predicted that I was going to be a blackjack dealer in a casino. I would not have believed them. I remember that in the old days, they used to call playing cards the Devil's Bible in Hungary."

In the old days, people considered a person who played card games fairly similar to an alcoholic. In their judgment, both persons had a disorder that could destroy their family lives.

"You are very lucky that you made it in America with your son at your side," one of my brothers commented, with a nod from my other brother.

"Yes, we did," I replied in agreement. "However, it was not an easy thing to do. It was certainly not due to any blind luck. We worked very hard. In the end, we were lucky that all that hard work paid off. I left Hungary because I became fed up with worrying about our political system, my ex-husband's exploits, and having to work two to three jobs at the same time just to pay for everything we needed. There were some other reasons as well."

In the early eighties, Hungary was under a corrupt and oppressive Communist dictatorship as a client state of what was then the Soviet Union. It was during this time that I left Hungary for good.

Following my departure from Hungary, major reforms took place that created a democratic country with a free-market economy. In October 1989, the Hungarian Communist Party convened its last congress and adopted legislation providing for multiparty parliamentary elections and a direct presidential election. This legislation transformed Hungary from a People's Republic into the Republic of Hungary, which now guaranteed human and civil rights, and created an institutional structure that ensured separation of powers among the judicial, executive, and legislative branches of government. In effect, Hungary reinvented itself in the image of Western European democracies.

"Yet it makes me sad to see so many homeless people here in Hungary," I continued. "It appears that all the political freedoms and market reforms of the last two and a half decades did not create the kind of prosperity that people had envisioned."

"At least we have more opportunities than before," Steven responded. "Talented people can now find ways to live better. Also we have a lot more new building projects and economic investment than ever before."

I will never feel like a stranger in my old country, because Budapest is my birthplace and it will always be close to my heart. Yet there are things that made me worried and sad about the current state of affairs in Hungary.

Growing up in Hungary, I had a decent middle-class family existence. My family and I lived in the suburbs of Budapest, in an area full of large homes with even larger gardens. In some ways, our part of the city was similar to a small town. Neighbors knew one another by their first names. The three biggest activities in our neighborhood were cooking competitions, gardening competitions, and gossip. Admittedly, some in the neighborhood could be a bit nosy.

My mother was a schoolteacher, and my father was an agronomist. They were wonderful and dedicated people. They lived for their family—for their three children: Steven, Andy, and I. We were always at the top of their list.

We had a very large garden, which my father called Our Eden. It had lots of big trees and lovely plants, some of which were of a special variety. My father, as an agronomist, collected these for fun. My parents also grew some vegetables in our garden for our daily use. As part of his work, my father would visit country farms to see how the various crops were doing in the fields. Many times, he would bring us home little animals from his travels to faraway farms. Taking care of our pets would keep us kids happy and occupied.

I learned to be responsible in my early youth. My parents made me responsible for my two younger brothers, who were always up to some mischief. I was only a couple of years older than my brothers but not necessarily better behaved. I also liked to climb trees, kick the ball in the dirt, and ride fast on a horse or on a bicycle. It was a double delight to climb on a cherry or apple tree and taste their fresh fruits whenever they were in season and my mom would ask us to pick some for supper.

Most importantly, I watched over my brothers like a dragon, as they referred to me at that time. I did not let anybody talk bad about them, although I would occasionally smack them when they misbehaved and would not listen to me. I also used to help my mom with household chores, including cooking.

When I arrived in Budapest to visit with my brother Steven, he also remembered these old days. As my plane landed, there was a big apocalyptic storm, with lots of thunder and lightning at the airport in Budapest. All of us were anxious to get home quickly from the airport and get some rest.

"When you wrote to us that you were coming, we bought you a new mattress to sleep on from the Dragon Shopping Center," Steven told me jokingly. "We hope that you will be comfortable during your visit."

"How nice of you to remember my childhood dragon nickname, which you gave me," I told him in response. Then I pointed out his car window. "Look, the dragon arrived in style, with thunder and lightning."

We were both laughing and talking about our childhood.

As a child, I liked to try on my mother's dresses and put on her lipstick secretly. When I was all made up, I would posture in front of the mirror and sing songs. On one occasion, my mom caught my performance; however, she waited until I finished my song.

"Bravo, prima donna!" she told me. "I see what you have been up to, my little diva. Can't you find something better to do? Go and look after your brothers!"

I was embarrassed. I ran away from my mom to look for my brothers, who usually played ball on the quiet street in the front of our house or liked to exchange toys and stamps with kids from the neighborhood.

One day after school, we decided with my girlfriend Edith to cut our long hair very short. To go to a hairstylist never crossed our mind. We just wanted to get it done quickly.

At the time, the length of my hair already passed my waistline. It was too much trouble to take care of it. I was also bored by it. It also bothered both Edith and me that our parents wanted us to keep our long locks braided.

My girlfriend chopped off my long hair with her big scissors at her house, and I did the same for her. Our long locks were now on her kitchen floor. Following our silly acts, we were afraid to see our parents again.

My girlfriend escorted me home because she knew that my father was very strict. When my father saw our haircuts, he could not be angry because we looked ridiculous with our messy short hair. He just started to laugh. He did not punish me.

"Your hair will grow back," he told me. "But right now, it does not look so good. Next time, you'd better go to a professional in a salon."

Each time the truck of the garbage collection services came to our street, which was usually in the morning before school, my two brothers, in their freshly pressed clean clothes, ran off to assist the workers. By the time my mom would go searching for them, they were already at the far end of our street, looking like a couple of chimney sweeps from all the dust and dirt. Of course, they did not receive any compensation for their services in collecting the garbage except in the form of my mom's anger. She was also angry with me, because I failed to report their activities.

My younger brother, Andy, once stopped a big horse when that horse tried to run away from the wagon it was pulling. At that time, he was only eight years old. Frightened by what they saw, our neighbors were shouting to my mother. You could hear the fear in their voices. Luckily, nothing happened to Andy.

On another occasion, my two young brothers tried to brand each other on the forehead with our red-hot iron fireplace poker. Apparently they were inspired by some adventure movie. Fortunately, my mom had caught them just in time, before they could go through with their plan.

Andy also brought home a lot of homeless or runaway dogs that he had found on the street on his way home from school.

"I swear that this time, this dog is a purebred!" he would confidently tell our incredulous mother. "The dogcatcher surely would not appreciate this wonderful dog and would put him right to sleep."

"The poor little guy," Steven then would usually say, to increase our odds of keeping the dog. "He is so cute. Hopefully, Mom, you will not chase him away to face a cruel fate, to wander the streets hungry and homeless."

My mom then had the headache of trying to figure out how to get rid of all these newfound purebred dogs without hurting our feelings. We certainly could not afford to run a dog shelter for all the neighborhood dogs.

My brothers often competed with me in all kinds of things like who could run fastest to our home's entrance, who could eat the soup for lunch the fastest, who could throw the ball highest, and so on. Of course, when the ball ended up breaking our neighbor's window, nobody was too happy. When something like this would happen, my mom would tell us that we would not get any spare change that week nor be allowed to go to the movies that weekend.

One day, one of our neighbors gave Andy a small cactus as a gift. Andy did not have a bag with him in which to carry the cactus home, so he just casually put the cactus inside his shirt. Following such an ill-advised move, it was my job to remove all the cactus thorns from Andy's chest that afternoon.

All three of us enjoyed looking after old Joe's donkey cart, which he normally parked in the front of the only pub in our neighborhood. On the way home from school, we would usually see the cart standing in front of the tavern. We would politely ask old Joe, who was usually so inebriated by that time that he could not even add two plus two anymore, whether he would let us drive his donkey cart home. He always said yes. We were very proud of ourselves holding the donkey's reins and guiding the donkey home, and luckily, the donkey already knew his way home.

"It is easier to guard a bag of fleas than the three of you," my poor mother used to tell us in exasperation. Yet years later, these childhood stories became cherished memories for my mother and even for some of our neighbors.

No one during our childhood would have predicted that all three of us, the little rascals of the neighborhood, would someday become professionals who were entrusted with a lot more responsibility than driving home the donkey cart. Steve became a doctor of medicine and, then, a director of a hospital. Andy became a lawyer in the United States. I was an attorney in Hungary before I moved to the States.

Finally, we were together again at Steve's house, in the garden, talking about old adventures. By this time, Attila had also arrived. Attila was the same age as us. He now worked as the head of a large corporation that he also owned. He also fondly recalled our childhood stories. We all laughed about all our childhood antics.

He reminded us about another incident involving Andy's cactus collection. One day it happened that my father tripped and fell on the biggest cactus that Andy had collected. My father was shouting for help. The thorns of the cactus had pricked his bottom. We were not at home. Attila, our friend, came over from next door to his rescue. All of this would not have happened if one of us had not inadvertently left a broomstick on the ground, obscured by the leaves of the bushes, next to the walkway, which had caused my poor father to fall.

Our friend then also fondly recalled his grandmother's cooking and how he and his brother always played practical jokes on her, so that she would think that they did not know how to behave well.

"If my grandmother were still alive, she would cook for us for sure, and we would all hug her," Attila said.

Attila and his brother would try to hide and secretly smoke cigarettes. Their favorite hiding place was the small water meter closet in their garden, near their home's entrance. One time, as Attila's father had just returned home from work, he saw smoke billowing out at the top crack of the door of that closet. He opened the door, and he saw Attila and his brother trying to hide their packs of cigarettes, cowering in fear.

"You do not have to hide them from me," Attila's dad told them. "But you will destroy your health with these cigarettes for sure."

Attila and my brothers then talked about our years in school. We all recalled that during Hungary's Communist era, the school required that all of us young students march with our classmates on each May 1. These marches were held at Heroes' Square, Budapest, to honor the Communist regime and International Workers' Day, a holiday aggressively promoted by communists and socialists.

During these marches, our school required all of us to shout at the top of our lungs, "Long live, long live Comrade Rákosi!" or we would get in big trouble.

We hated May 1. We not only needed to be at the march on Heroes' Square, but we also had to get there on foot. In Hungary, May could already be hot. Yet we would be marched about two miles in that heat from our school just to get to Heroes' Square.

Along the way, we were required to loudly shout the regime's phony hurrah. We truly hated these forced marches.

Mátyás Rákosi of Hungary was a terrible dictator, who modeled himself after Stalin. Rákosi described himself as "Stalin's best Hungarian disciple" or "Stalin's best pupil." At the height of his rule, Rákosi developed a strong cult of personality around himself. Yet he had nothing to brag about. Hungary was economically devastated and ruled by a small group of corrupt and cruel Communists. American journalist John Gunther described Rákosi as "the most malevolent character I ever met in political life."

164

All of us lived in fear of the regime. Hungary's State Protection Authority (Hungarian: Allamvedelmi Hatosag or "AVH") was the secret police force of Hungary until 1956. It was conceived of as an external appendage of the Soviet secret police or KGB and its predecessor entities, including the MGB. In the end, the AVH succeeded in attaining its own indigenous reputation for great brutality in Hungary during a series of horrific and bloody purges.

On many nights, the AVH would come in secret for someone, and that person would never be seen alive again. Their actions and methods were like those of the Soviet secret police. It was being whispered then, and more recently was confirmed in news reports, that among other things, the AVH utilized an extralarge meat grinder to kill people before their remains were thrown into the Danube River. In this manner, the Danube witnessed many horrific moments of Hungarian history.

Attila's father was one of the AVH's many victims. He was a mechanical engineer. A malicious neighbor made a false report about him to the AVH and claimed that Attila's dad was working on a small atomic bomb in his basement.

The AVH then quickly picked up Attila's dad, along with his drawings of a new machine that he had been working on. Members of the AVH then beat him until he suffered a heart attack. Following repeated beatings, his drawings were finally looked at by the prosecutor's office.

Looking at the drawings, the prosecutor realized that Attila's father was completely innocent. There was no atomic bomb. So the prosecutor ordered that the AVH was to let Attila's father go free. When Attila's father finally came home, he suffered yet another heart attack from all the stress and mistreatment by the AVH. A couple of days later, he died.

The Hungarian AVH similarly mistreated my father. My father's misfortune came about because of jealousy at his work. At the time, my father received a valuable promotion, but his friend and colleague did not. The wife of my father's friend then became very envious of my father's success at work. She decided to use an old letter that my father had written a decade earlier against my father.

At the time, my father and his friend who did not get the promotion at work had already known each other for many years. During World War II, my father was required to serve on the Russian Front. From the front, he wrote a letter to his friend, which his friend and his wife apparently kept for years. In the letter, he, among other things, wrote that "It is bad enough that we have to fight with the Germans, but now everybody hates us. Even these cursed partisans are taking shots at us."

Before the war, the Kingdom of Hungary relied on increased trade with the neighboring countries of Fascist Italy and Nazi Germany to pull itself out of the Great Depression. Additionally, Hungary hoped to benefit territorially from its relationship with such Axis powers in its efforts to regain those territories that it had lost during World War I.

As such, in 1940, under pressure from Germany, Hungary joined the Axis. In 1941, Hungarian forces participated in the invasion of Yugoslavia and the invasion of the Soviet Union. Hitler, however, knew that Hungary was not an enthusiastic participant in the Axis coalition. As such, by 1944, German forces decided that they needed to occupy Hungary to ensure its loyalty to Germany.

Following World War II and the defeat of Nazi Germany, Soviet troops took over as Hungary's new masters and colonizers. The Russians then systematically went after those who had anti-Soviet or anti-Communist sentiments.

As a result of Soviet backing, Rákosi was installed as the head of the Hungarian government, along with the AVH as his muscle, to run the country with an iron fist. Many members of the Communist regime were strong sympathizers of the Soviet partisans who had, indeed, fought valiantly on the Russian Front against Germany and her allies. Following World War II, all of those who were even suspected of being opponents of the

Soviet-backed regime or its elements, like former partisans, were brutally oppressed.

For his letter, which the wife of my father's friend delivered to the hands of the AVH, my father was deported. First, members of the AVH brutally beat my father. Then the AVH had my father deported to the Russian border of Hungary, where he had to work in a labor camp for three years, for which he received starvation wages. All of this happened because of a letter that my father wrote during the war in which he had not shown enthusiasm about partisans who were shooting at his military unit.

We were lucky that he was not killed or deported to Siberia. Yet these three years were the hardest. During this time, my mom and my siblings lived separately in our home in Budapest. We could not survive on the starvation wages that my father received and relied on produce from our garden and on the goodness of our friends and relatives to try to survive.

We also talked about the happier times with Attila.

We recalled our favorite dog, Muffy, who would pull our sled during the winters when we had heavy snow in front of our houses. Muffy was a puli. The puli is a small-medium breed of Hungarian herding dog known for its long, corded coat. The tight curls of the coat, similar to dreadlocks, make it virtually waterproof or snow-proof, like a high-tech sweater.

We also remembered that at one time, my two brothers invited Attila and his brother to climb a tall tree near our house, so that Attila and his brother could secretly sneak a peek through the high bathroom window and see me bathing. Their mischievous invitation was, of course, unbeknownst to me. Suddenly, one of them fell down with a loud thud from the tree. Then my mother showed up with her cooking spoon. It was made from heavy dense wood. She never spanked us with it. The mere sight of the spoon was enough.

Some of their stories I heard for the first time, because I was on vacation. For example, I never knew that my brother Andy came home one day from school in a fancy funeral hearse.

"Who died?" my poor mom asked, frightened when she saw the black hearse pull up in front of our home.

"No one we knew," my brother responded cheerfully as he climbed out of the hearse. "I could not get a ride home from school, and the decedent did not make any objections to a quick stop at my house on his way to the funeral parlor."

Attila, my brothers, and I also recalled all the talented people that left Hungary during the Hungarian Revolution of 1956, including a lot of scientists, doctors, and artists, as well as those who took part in the revolution. Hungary's Golden Team or the Mighty Magyars, our country's all-star soccer team, also left Hungary around that time, and Hungarian soccer has never recovered.

At the time, no one knew that Russia's "friendship," or more correctly forty-year military occupation of Hungary, would come to an end in 1989.

Thousands of people fought and died in 1956 to end the Russian oppression. No one came to our help.

During the revolution, Hungary, with its ten million citizens, faced down the might of the Soviet Empire, with its two hundred million citizens. While Soviet Russia was already a superpower at the time, Hungary had a very limited number of weapons.

Faced with such impossible odds, many ordinary people and young men risked their lives and fought valiantly in the streets. If captured, many of them were shot on the spot. In its revolution, the odds were clearly against Hungary. Decades later, we still remembered how painful and unjust it was to face Russian brutality and oppression.

During the Hungarian Revolution of 1956, Radio Free Europe, a radio broadcast organization sponsored by the US government, encouraged rebels to fight and suggested that Western support was imminent. Yet these broadcasts did not reflect President Eisenhower's decision that the United States would not provide military support for the revolution. Notwithstanding, the broadcaster made announcements such as "Hold out and fight, Hungarian people; the United States will come and help you."

Of course, these statements turned out to be empty promises. Even the Hungarian military, led by Paul Maleter, joined the Hungarian rebels against Soviet occupation. They valiantly held out until their last bullet against the Russians. They were all executed.

Russia violently repressed the Hungarian Revolution. Russian troops arrived in Hungary with an endless line of tanks and even special forces. We only learned later that the Russian troops were already at the Hungarian border, and they were waiting for their chance to march in. The situation was not all that dissimilar from what happened in the Ukraine in 2014 and beyond.

Some of the Russians did not even know what the fighting was all about because their leaders did not tell them the truth. They were misled. Many of them thought they were fighting against fascism; they did not know they were fighting against Hungary's freedom. Again, our situation was not all that dissimilar from what happened in the Ukraine in 2014 and beyond.

During the 1956 Hungarian Revolution, I hid under my parents' bed. I was a very small child. The sound of gunshots scared me, especially, the sound of cannon shots. One day, I saw the lifeless body of our neighbor's uncle on our neighbor's porch. On another day, a man standing near my mother and me on the street suddenly collapsed next to the door of the bakery. There were shots fired in all directions.

The rumble of armored vehicles stressed us out because we did not know if one of them would stop in front of our house. These were very tragic times.

In the end, Russian forces engaged in mass retaliation on the population, which had many more victims. This was one of the reasons that about a quarter of a million people left Hungary immediately following the revolution, with hundreds of thousands more following in their footsteps thereafter.

In addition to the conflict, many people also chose to emigrate to the West because the Communist system was already a proven failure. Communist leaders made many empty promises and, with the crushing of all opposition, made even more enemies. It was great that the West was prepared to take in Hungary's political refugees. Our people's departure, however, was sad for those members of their families who had been left behind in Hungary.

Following the revolution, the leadership of Hungary's Communist Party made all kinds of bold promises relative to future prosperity. However, these promises were made without any real substance behind them. They quoted Marx that, in the West, they would merely become the exploited tools of capitalists. Yet they forgot to tell them that in Hungary, they would remain exploited tools of the Soviets.

Their empty promises remind me of the story of the wizard who promised to the sultan that he would teach the sultan's donkey to speak.

In the story, the wizard met the old sultan, and the sultan asked him, "People tell me that you know everything and can do anything. Can you teach my donkey how to speak?"

"Yes, Your Excellency," the wizard answered. "I will be able to teach the donkey how to speak within twenty-five years. But you will have to give me fifty thousand dinars."

"I will give you what you ask, but if you don't teach the donkey how to speak, I will chop off your head," the sultan replied.

Time went on, and the wizard lived happily and had lots of fun on the sultan's account. But his friends would ask him, "When are you going to teach the donkey to speak?"

The wizard answered, "Never! Because in twenty-five years, either the sultan or the donkey will be dead. Who knows? Maybe even I might die by then. For now, I will enjoy my money!"

The wizard's promises in the story resembled the promises of the Communist leaders in Hungary following the revolution. They often said, "Your children will be happy and will have a bright future. When you follow your wise leaders, Hungarians, in the future, shall not want for anything. Human life and human dignity are of the highest importance for our regime."

It was, of course, difficult to believe such empty words after what most people had just experienced. And where are these phony leaders now? Did they fulfill their promises?

Of course they did not. Instead, they stole from all of us. Even when Communism collapsed and Hungary was no longer under Russian rule, these leaders sold what they could to Western investors and stuffed their own pockets in the process, as one of my friends told me who stayed behind and witnessed these tragic events.

Even under a free-market economy, there are now still just too many homeless people and unemployed. Most of that is attributable to incompetence, lack of social cohesion, and corruption.

Throughout history, Hungary's leaders were often other stronger nations' puppets. These so-called leaders did not unite the general population and lead them to a better future. Instead, most of them were corrupt and power-hungry; they did not care to act responsibly, and only cared about their own pleasures.

In recent history, the Treaty of Trianon dealt the first major blow to Hungary. The Treaty of Trianon was a peace agreement of 1920 to formally end World War I among most of the Allies of World War I, including France and Britain, and the Axis powers, including the Kingdom of Hungary.

The Treaty of Trianon was extremely harsh on Hungary and unjustifiably one-sided. The resulting treaty cost Hungary an unprecedented two-thirds of her territory and over one half of her total population. Add to this the loss of all her seaports, up to 90 percent of her vast natural resources, industry, railways, and other infrastructure. Millions of Hungarians saw borders arbitrarily redrawn around them.

In addition to this disastrous treaty, World War I, World War II, and the Hungarian Revolution of 1956 each caused incalculable devastation to the country. Hungary, with its remaining ten million people, with its weak leaders, weak remaining finances, and weak remaining industry, were swept aside by the great powers for many years. Neither the West nor Russia cared about Hungary's future. Each wanted to use the region for its own purposes.

Yet most Hungarians continued to eagerly yearn not just for true democracy, but also to be united with the rest of Europe. In 2004, Hungary was admitted as a member state of the European Union, or EU for short. Since Hungary became a member state of the European Union, things have changed; however, some things did not improve or got worse.

Most of the factories in Hungary were acquired and then quickly closed down by competing firms from the West, who wanted to protect their own market share and their own domestic labor markets back home. Given such protectionist machinations coming from the West, Hungary's current outlook in terms of industrial development remains bleak. Yet the entrepreneurial milieu is still strong, and those in business maintain a positive outlook.

There have been many other challenges. The jury is still out on whether Hungary has achieved true democracy. While there have been social activist and community organizers who have attempted to sow the seeds of a durable democracy by having an informed electorate and a more liberal society, they did not quite succeed.

Most people in the region still have their mind-set stuck in the past, failing to learn from the lessons of our thousand-year shared history. Many others think that change will happen by itself or through the political process alone. Hopefully, they will realize that change for the better will only come through hard work by all, cooperation with all, and the continuous fight for justice for all.

Whenever the country faced difficult times, those individuals who have demonstrated a deep love for Hungary and placed their country and its people first were, in the end, instrumental to its survival. It is, of course, hard to change hearts and minds at once, when many were born under a different political era, an era that had absolute rule and great divisiveness. Such mistakes should not be repeated.

Lately, Russia has started to reengage in Hungary, in large part as a part of furthering its gas pipeline interests in Europe. Russia signed several trade agreements with Hungary. Many people in Hungary do not trust in the appropriate implementation of these trade agreements with Russia because of recent developments in the Ukraine and other political issues in Russia. In addition, as Hungary was forced to learn in 1956, a friendship with Russia can quickly turn out for the worst.

Recently, Russian President Vladimir Putin stirred even further controversy when he paid tribute to Soviet soldiers killed in Hungary, including those that killed Hungarian freedom fighters during Russia's bloody suppression of the 1956 Hungarian Revolution. Yet Hungarian law states that anyone "justifying the crimes committed by the Communist system is to be punished." This means that Putin's commemoration of those Russian soldiers that killed Hungarian patriots violated Hungarian law.

Yet according to one video available on YouTube, the Russian president has shown even further contempt to Hungary and its current president, Victor Orban, in one recent interview with a Hungarian journalist.

"How do you respond," the reporter asked Putin, "to our President Victor Orban's claim that Mr. Orban was the one who chased out the Russians from Hungary?"

Hearing the reporter's question, Mr. Putin began to laugh uncontrollably.

"Do not make me laugh," Putin then said. "He could not have said that. The last time Mr. Orban was visiting me in Russia, there was a 'drip' and 'drip' sound. It turned out that he had shit himself down to his ankle."

It is unbelievable that someone in Mr. Putin's position could afford to engage in such vulgarity. I find it especially cynical. According to some news accounts, Mr. Putin can afford to be dismissive to Mr. Orban, as Russia has been helping to finance the far right movement that Mr. Orban's regime represents.

Many people in Hungary told me that "We had always hoped for something better; instead, some of our newly elected leaders created more problems for our country than all the wars put together."

In fact, no country can achieve long-term stability without creating the foundations for a stable economy, which includes collaboration at home and with other nations. Of course, such collaboration should be with nations that are stable themselves. I do not think that anybody with a responsible mind would want to team up with any aggressors.

Sadly, even in this modern era, Hungarian politicians did not unite the citizens of Hungary. Instead, they continue to divide people based on ethnicity and background. Minority groups, such as Romani, Jews, ethnic minorities, and migrants, are too often victims of discrimination. Regardless of the oppressive rationalizations, it should not be allowed to occur. All forms of discrimination should end.

Even more appalling is that certain members of the Jobbik party are even willing to go as far as to engage in violence, brutality, and worse on the basis of race or ethnicity. Too many such infamous acts of violence can be found by reading the press releases in Budapest and elsewhere.

Jobbik is the shortened version of the Movement for a Better Hungary (Hungarian: Jobbik Magyarországért Mozgalom). It is a Hungarian radical ultranationalist political party. The party describes itself as "a principled, conservative and radically patriotic Christian party," whose "fundamental purpose" is the protection of "Hungarian values and interests."

Yet in June 2007, an individual supported by Jobbik founded and registered the organization called Magyar Gárda or "Hungarian Guard." The mission of the Hungarian Guard included "maintaining public order." The Hungarian Guard's uniform was composed of black boots, black trousers with white shirt, black vest with the shape of a lion on its back and a coat of arms on the front, a shielded black cap, and a red-and-white striped scarf. Until ultimately banned, it reminded one of the horrific fascist group the Arrow Cross during World War II.

According, to one recent report by Harvard University, during the last five years in Hungary, the establishment of such vigilante groups and hate crimes against Roma and other minority groups have also been accompanied by a climate of increasing social and economic exclusion.

Shortly after the regime changed to a representative democracy in Hungary, most of the mental institutions in Budapest closed. As a result, today, many of their patients run free on the streets, even though many represent a grave danger not only to themselves but also to the public at large. Some perhaps even join hate groups.

The issues with mental health in Hungary and the United States are similar. In Hungary, most mental hospitals have been empty for years. They do not have enough funding to care for the mentally ill. There are some hospitals with mental services, but far short of the level of actual services desperately needed.

Sadly, most people do not realize that mental illness can happen to anyone, following a serious head injury or as a secondary consequence of certain illnesses. Mental illness is the result of birth defects only in some cases. Regardless, we'd better make sure that help is always available for the mentally ill.

A couple of years ago, one of my friends in Hungary told me that she needed to buy and take with her medication to the hospital, as otherwise she would not receive full treatment; the hospital would not be able to provide her with even basic medication. Still, she was very happy to be able to get a hospital bed. She had bladder cancer.

She also told me that modern instruments for treatment are placed in the hospital basements because nobody can use them. Yet the old instruments they have are imprecise, as she was informed upon her arrival at the hospital. So if she wanted to get treatment with the hospital's old instruments, she was taking a real risk that the radiation treatment would cause more damage to her living tissues than just killing the cancer cells. This was the reason that she could not get proper localized radiation therapy. Six months later, she died.

Before she died, we often spoke by telephone. Once she told me that "Hungary would have been much better off if it had used its limited resources to build modern hospitals and schools, instead of a sports arena, in the tiny hometown of our prime minister in the middle of nowhere."

Prior to her death, my friend's doctor counseled her that he could not provide her with more modern irradiation methods.

"It is a shame," her doctor told her, "that we do not have the money to pay to a trained nurse to handle the new instruments needed, which would provide a more precise irradiation."

My friend, however, was not aware that the use of such a machine would be her only realistic alternative to stop the progress of her deadly disease. She continued to take her cancer medications, but sadly, these were not strong enough to kill the cancer cells.

When I heard about her situation, I cried. I found it very sad that she was not able to receive the proper treatment that she desperately needed, notwithstanding that we live in such a modern era even in Hungary.

In Hungary, the population now enjoys a free democratic society. In fact, there is now so much freedom that people are even allowed to dig their own graves in public cemeteries, with the help of their friends or relatives, if they do not have enough money to pay for their own funeral services.

This is not a joke. It is a newly enacted law. However, having such a self-service funeral is not a great accomplishment of freedom that any society should be proud to proclaim.

Of course, the Hungarian government is intent on solving all societal problems, but a weak economy and fewer resources provide less opportunity for meaningful solutions. When the economy was converted to free-market capitalism, those who were in charge sold everything mostly for the benefit of their own pocketbooks. To begin with, these companies were already not in great shape, and many of them are still barely hanging on today.

Instead of creating a positive environment and having help available to cope with the transition, the government only instituted stricter laws and regulations, especially against migrants, homeless, and the criminal element.

At the same time, many home mortgages in Hungary were pegged to foreign currencies, so when the exchange rates became bad, banks were able to increase interest rates on existing mortgages from 5 to 25 percent, with many families losing their ability to cope with such large increases. Many became homeless.

The banks' change in interest rates came suddenly and without prior notice. Nobody could stop it, and nobody could do anything about it—even though it seemed very unfair.

Regardless of the high aspirations one has for democracy and free markets, as practiced, such systems were not flawless in Hungary. The government drafted a new constitution and enacted many new laws intended to benefit those who are in power. Indeed, those in power do not want to have effective checks and balances in the Hungarian Constitution. Instead, corruption and nepotism are the ruling principles. It is a system that favors the few to the detriment of the many.

At the same time, the European Union is also not helpful. Its requirements often are contrary to the best interests of Hungary and make things more complicated. It is also, however, a problem that Hungary has borrowed heavily, and the money it borrowed was not spent in ways that were consistent with the conditions of the European Union.

"We do not let other nations dictate for us" is a phrase sometimes heard in the Hungarian Parliament.

"Why did you then borrow all this money subject to all these restrictions?" is the retort sometimes given. "Now you are responsible to spend it in accordance with their requirements and to pay it back as required!"

The other reason that Hungary is not popular in the European Union could be that the union disapproves of the Hungarian government's treatment of certain minorities, its apparent corruption, and its competing trade agreements with Russia. As the saber rattling is ongoing over the situation in the Ukraine, Hungary's further attempt to cozy up to Russia is indeed problematic. It could have very negative consequences in the end. Sadly, I have seen many tricks of politics used in Hungary that in the end did not end so well for my old country.

The European Union is slow and uncoordinated in its response to the migrant crisis as well. The migrants from Syria and other countries in the Middle East have been arriving daily by thousands to Hungary, and the country was not ready to process them. Because they arrived unexpectedly and in great numbers, the system has been unable to handle all of them.

It has become an overwhelming issue for Hungary. Among these migrants were indeed some who turned out to be terrorists. Many are arriving without birth certificates or any official papers, and their identity cannot be determined.

There are many migrants in my old country from Iraq, Syria, Afghanistan, and other countries in that region. They want to find refuge there and elsewhere in Europe. Many want to travel on to Germany, but the government in Hungary was not appropriately responsive in the way that it addressed the issue.

This is not something new. Sadly, in Hungary, the government is ineffective in dealing with almost all domestic problems—they could not even help their own citizens. There are many unemployed and homeless people, especially in the capital.

The Hungarian government does not have the ability nor the institutions to help their own people, let alone the experience or the money to handle such a huge number of migrants. At the same time, they are unwilling to provide a lot of help, as they are worried that it would only encourage more migrants to come. Instead, they quickly built a fence at the country's southern border. And when the border was enforced by aggressive police tactics, it only created unnecessary antagonism.

"Our leaders should have much better cooperation with other European nations to deal with these issues," my friend Clara, who lives in Hungary, said to me. "They also need to have much better organization to handle the matter and not create an atmosphere of discrimination. A thoughtful and cooperative approach would be more helpful to manage these migrants, instead of a gut reaction. For sure, this issue has been a major challenge for all European countries, not only for Hungary. Our country was certainly not prepared for that many people to come through. Yet most average Hungarians helped the migrants, even though they could face a criminal citation, and even jail, from their government for doing so."

At the same time, some countries that are neighbors to Hungary blame Hungary for the issues presented by the migrants. Many countries do not want to assist the migrants at all. In the end, even Germany and Austria placed limitations on the number of migrants they would allow in, as the migrants were arriving by the thousands each week.

"The news stories are now full of negative things and comments," my friend Peter, who also still lives in Hungary, said to me. "Even the Austrians, our next-door neighbors, say very negative things about Hungary. Yet just recently, they got caught for dumping garbage in Hungary with their eighteen-wheeler trucks. And, of course, they really exploited us during the Habsburg era. Remember? Their ruler, the kaiser, also ruled over Hungary with an iron fist, all the way until the conclusion of World War I."

Indeed, prior to World War I, Hungary was a vassal state of the Astro-Hungarian Empire, with the ruling class primarily comprised of Viennese (Austrians) and their favorites.

"I do remember," I responded to Peter. "I am very sorry that the democracy did not bring prosperity, even after we got rid of the Austrians and then the Russians. Hungary still struggles, and there are still many injustices. As we know, times change, and people do too, but not fast enough and not always for the better. Hopefully, things will change, and democracy will prevail with the cooperation of all the people."

Yet I am saddened by all that is still going wrong. Why is Hungary still left in such a negative position and still seen in such a negative light?

"Mainly because we are at the frontier of the Schengen Area," another friend of mine commented, who also still lives in Hungary. "Things are not going according to our choice; rather, they are dictated by the necessity of the war on terror and its consequences, which have reverberated in the Middle East and now in Europe. Not to mention that everything happened so fast, and its scope and size were truly unexpected. Many of our people were shocked and did not know how to react."

The Schengen Area is an area comprising twenty-six Western and Central European countries that have abolished passport and any other type of border control at their common borders, also referred to as internal borders. It mostly functions as a single country for international travel purposes, with a common visa policy. Hungary is at the southern border of the Schengen Area, where most migrants often tend to cross into Western Europe.

Yet most migrants have been too scared to register with authorities in Hungary, because officials would put in their paperwork that they arrived illegally. Based on the rules of the Schengen Area, Western European nations will reject those who entered illegally anywhere (without permission); at best, they would have to stay put in the country where they entered.

It is sad that migrants are often treated so harshly, because when you are escaping bombs and bullets, you do not have time to ask for permission. Yet given the many places of origin for these migrants and that they often lack paperwork, it will be difficult to know who truly escaped from a war zone and who is merely looking for opportunity.

In any event, most migrants do not want to be registered in Hungary. They would rather flee from the Hungarian police. Indeed, Hungarian officials should not put into their database negative comments about migrants unless they have good reason to believe that people who are identified in such manner are terrorists.

Migrants most often just want to quickly travel on to Western Europe. Several volunteer organizations, such as the Red Cross, have been helping migrants in the refugee camps. Many Hungarians, private citizens, also have given food and other aid to migrants and have helped migrants travel on to the Austrian border.

All those private citizens in Hungary that assisted migrants in such a manner and continue to assist migrants are risking jail. At the same time, I feel ashamed to see articles in the news about some segments of the Hungarian population behaving heartlessly or worse toward migrants, including some members of the government, which, in some of these articles, brings up comparisons to the Nazi era. I feel that not all Hungarians should be blamed for the improper actions of these individuals.

A political one-liner I heard a long time ago in Hungary is that "We should not be concerned about our politicians, because our politicians certainly are not concerned about us." Unfortunately, this is still very true today.

Normal human beings have empathy for others. They try to help the less fortunate, not turn them away or punish them. A responsible government does not let a country's reputation drop into the toilet for financial reasons or for any other reasons.

Those Hungarians who left their country during earlier times are in pain and disappointment when they see all the negative news coverage relative to the poor treatment of migrants. They feel unhappy about life in Hungary and worry about the country's future.

Whenever I heard negative news coverage about Hungary, I felt as if someone wanted to visit harm on my mother. Yet I think that the truth should be reported. Only by admitting errors and faults will we be able to make needed positive change for the future.

The Kurt Lewin Foundation conducted a research study in Eastern Hungary for over a year. They examined the relationship between schools and democratic "active citizenship." Active citizenship means people getting involved in their local communities and democracy at all levels, from towns to cities to nationwide activity. Active citizenship can be as small as a campaign to clean up your street or as big as educating young people about democratic values, skills, and participation. Active citizenship is one of the most important steps toward healthy societies, especially in new democracies like Hungary.

The study found that, in general, students valued their relationship with their classmates, but less than half of the students are able to share their problems with their teachers.

Regarding minorities, the students did not express a high level of solidarity. They were disillusioned with politics, democracy, and social issues. Students prefer a less democratic, stronger-handed, more authoritarian approach. They are not interested in any of the political parties. Still, representatives of radical, extreme political views are generally more acceptable for them than mainstream political parties. Teachers, compared to students, find democratic values more important and are more likely to reject antidemocratic activity. Nonetheless, findings concerning teachers are also characterized by distrust and disappointment with regard to politics.

All of these findings are, of course, very troubling with regard to the political future of the country.

"Your country got what it deserves, because they did not appreciate our friendship," many of my Russian coworkers would tell me.

"We would have appreciated," I would respond, "except for the fact that your friendship came in the form of a dictatorship and exploitation of our country. We never had anything bad to say against the ordinary Russian people."

Sitting in my brother's garden, Attila, our friend, told us that he is happy most of the time, because his children are all successful and he is living very comfortably in his own big house.

"All of that is very good," I said to him, "but you are certainly one lucky exception."

"In today's society," Attila responded, "people fear one another far more than they fear the government."

"My heart goes out to all the people who are mistreated by their fellow citizens in a discriminatory manner," I told Attila and my brothers. "Discrimination is unjust in any form."

Sadly, the current situation in Hungary might change at any time for something even worse, especially given the Jobbik party's ongoing involvement in government affairs. Many individuals living in Hungary are scared on account of their ethnicity or political differences with that far-right organization.

In Hungarian, "Jobb" means "better" or "right"; however, in reality, Jobbik should be called "worse" or "wrong," as their extreme conduct has only made things a whole lot worse. They are a far-right organization. They instigated assaults and killings against members of minority groups. They do not respect the law or human rights. Even though those that commit such crimes may ultimately be convicted, it does not restore the lives of those individuals who unjustly perished at their hands.

"It is very sad, but Jobbik does not follow the law and they do not respect anybody," my friends in Hungary would often tell me. "However, there are problems with discrimination in other countries as well. People are not perfect in the United States either. Discrimination still persists in the United States, even though it is one of the most advanced countries in the world."

"I wish Hungarians would follow all the good examples of a civil society like the United States," I would tell them, "not all the worst conduct that can be found in the world."

If I had not seen the news reports and heard some of the stories firsthand, I would never have believed these things could happen among so many nice and educated people who live in my old country. However, many of them are reluctant or in fear to speak out.

My brother Andy has been a regular reader of the Bible.

"Mankind was always in trouble and did many horrifying things," he would often tell me. "I am just happy while I can have tasty food, great wine, and good company. It is enough for me to worry about my own family. I will let God and the politicians take care about the rest."

"In the future, I would like to remember only nice stories and about our happy childhood together," said Attila, "because politics are scary everywhere in the world."

Attila helped us recall our earlier adventures and happier times while the four of us sat together on my brother's terrace. Many years had passed since all of us had spent time together. We enjoyed the good wine and the peaceful environment of my brother's beautiful garden.

"It is usually easier to view things from a safe distance and criticize other people's shortcomings," my brother Steven said, "but it is not so easy to make things right. We have often solved impossible challenges in our country, but for some real wonders, we still have to wait."

"I would agree with you," I told him, "but who elected these kinds of political leaders in our country? I know that the majority of the people here are very nice and were duped by politicians; however, they also have some responsibility for their choices. They should elect leaders who unite the nation and do not let corruption and discrimination destroy the political system."

I would like to see my old country prosper. I would like to see my old country eliminate corruption, discrimination, and unemployment. I would like to see better cooperation with the European Union in the interest of a more humane treatment of the migrants. I hope that one day my dream will come true and Hungary will be free of its old and ugly ghosts, all of which are serious obstacles in its future development.

Recently, Hungary attracted a lot of negative reviews in the World Forum Foundation, as their stories and reports were more focused on the extremes than on the life of ordinary citizens. I believe that most Hungarians will continue to reject corruption and discrimination.

History has never favored weaker nations. Some countries got more than their fair share of miseries. Hungary's history, wars, and politics are full of misadventures; it is a story of endless fights and struggles. History indeed has always influenced every individual's destiny to a great extent in this part of the world.

Hungary has suffered more than most countries during the recent past. Given such episodes, it would be better if they would stop all factions that stir up trouble. To begin with, it would certainly be better for all if people would show more tolerance toward each other.

Discrimination has always existed all over the world, not just in Hungary. It is part of human history—a great disease. It is unjust and disgusting.

"I do not feel safe to travel to Budapest anymore, because too many negative events have happened there during the past ten years," one of my friends, who is a world-famous Roma (Gypsy) musician, told me. "Supporters of Jobbik exterminated a Roma family, including their children. They were upset that the money that the European Union provided for the education of the Roma population in Hungary was more than the portion that they received."

"I agree with your caution, and I am really devastated to hear of such tragic events," I told him. "However, please do not forget about all the nice things that we also lived through and all of those good people we have known in our country. Unfortunately, discrimination and horrific acts exist almost everywhere in the world. I think that we are no better and no worse than other nations."

Just a few weeks prior to this conversation, I was waiting in a very long line at Walmart Customer Service in Las Vegas. While the line was long, there was only one cashier behind that register. Approximately twenty people stood there for more than thirty minutes until more help finally arrived.

"This line is way too long for just one cashier," I blurted out with a sigh in my heavy Hungarian accent that still persists to this day.

"Why don't you then go back home where you came from if you do not like it?" an unknown woman who stood behind me in that line retorted sharply.

"I am at home, and I do not like it," I responded back to her.

All of human history is, of course, full of mistreatment of ethnic minorities and the disabled. Here are just a few examples. The ancient Spartans would throw babies that they perceived as either weak or puny off Mount Taygetos. Ancient Romans killed Christians en masse. ISIS is certainly attempting to do the same. In Japan, the ruling class discriminated against Burakumins, those with occupations considered impure or tainted by death (such as executioners, undertakers, workers in slaughterhouses, butchers, or tanners). Polpot, the crazed dictator of Cambodia, slaughtered most of his own nation, just as the Syrian government is doing today. The same thing happened in Sudan with all the ethnic cleansing. Not to mention Hitler, who was the worst of the worst. Yet these are just a few examples.

Even in the United States, which is clearly one of the best countries in the world, some still discriminate against blacks and migrants. While it is against the law, sadly, discrimination still exists.

Such prejudices and the actions influenced by them represent the dark side of humanity. They reflect negatively on the individuals who are doing it, and also cause a lot of emotional pain and disadvantage to those who are victimized by it. It is very sad that people do not look at their own flaws before they judge anybody and treat them so harshly. It seems that parts of humanity have still not learned from its troubled past.

"You are right, and I agree with you, but it is very painful for me what has happened and is still happening in Hungary," one of my friends told me.

"Scientists, mostly those who conduct DNA research, analyzed the evidence to determine where all of us come from. They wanted to know the origins of people and nations. They came to the conclusion that all Caucasians had at least one common ancestor during the last thousand years, and even members of other races are very closely related. In fact, we have all been cousins, and people have continually mixed on all continents. Even among Caucasians there is a likelihood that some of them have some recent African, Asian, or other race or ethnicity in their DNA. Is it not ridiculous and sad that discrimination still exists?" I asked one of my old friends in Hungary. "I think that it would be more appropriate to judge each person based on his or her own merits and not put any group of people under a collective label."

"Given that so many suffered unjustly," my friend told me, "it is certainly time to eliminate discrimination. I am really sorry for the Roma race, for example, who were often mistreated in Hungary. Many of them deserve a better life."

"I agree," I responded. "I am also sorry that the democracy in Hungary has not found a way to bring prosperity. There are also many confused people, especially those who have been misled by false prophets."

Indeed, the majority of Hungarians are well educated, talented, and kindhearted people. Even during World War II, many of them helped Jewish people escape Nazi persecution, risking their own lives in the process. Today, they still help the unfortunate migrants from Syria, even though they face the threat of prosecution and jail from their government.

There are also many people in Hungary who do not like discrimination in their home nation; however, they are afraid of the Jobbik party.

Usually, most people are ill informed about European history. They do not know, for example, that Hitler's forces occupied Hungary and all the worst atrocities were committed, not by choice, but under the direct orders of the Fuhrer and under the control of his military. Yet Hungary is still judged the same as the leading fascists of that era.

Unfortunately, the popular media, including movies and news reports, have only reported on Hungary's negative past, without adequately focusing on the suffering endured by the populace for many decades under Communist rule, for example. Hungary, as a small country, was mostly used and abused during its history. That perception of unfairness from neighbors can perhaps explain at least some of the roots of discrimination that persist. Most people have lost their trust and are reluctant to look for ways to cooperate. Yet they need to wake up soon and realize that this is a wrong path.

The many accomplished Hungarians, heroes, inventors, risk takers, and Nobel Prize winners are rarely reported upon, yet there are so many. They are, of course, forgotten for understandable reasons. These positive facts are all forgotten because the new political regime that currently exists in Hungary is not fighting effectively enough against prejudice. Instead, it is only emphasizing the importance of the Hungarian race to the exclusion of others. Sadly, to maintain their grip on power, many in government are more interested in putting to work the old Roman principle of *divide et impera,* or divide and rule.

Yet to have a more successful future, governments should help those who have to struggle for survival and unite all of society so that everybody feels invested in building a better future. Each person should feel that all of them are rowing in the same boat.

Human life is precious regardless of background or skin color, yet some governments do not care enough about the misery of the oppressed unless people revolt. The world would surely be a better place if all children could grow up happy and all of us could live always in peace and empathy toward one another.

Budapest is the capital of Hungary. It is a beautiful city. Its beauty and its greatness were made possible by the hard work of many. Its beauty also resides in the hearts of those many good people that live there. I am reminded of Katy Perry's *Fireworks* video filmed around Budapest, with interspersed scenes of young people becoming confident in themselves.

I felt it necessary to write about my thoughts for the preservation of the best part of Hungary's history. Yet the current political situation in my old country shattered me. I would like to be proud of my old country, without any shame. I want to believe that, as I have always known to be the case, people there will continue to help those that are less fortunate. Hopefully, good people who are responsible and courageous enough will look out for the future of Hungary and unite in the interest of a better future for all.

CHAPTER 16

STRATEGIES FOR DEALING WITH STRESS

In modern societies, stress affects our daily lives more at every level than almost any other factor, regardless of our age, race, or social status. Stress influences our daily lives, directly and indirectly, throughout our life span. When stress directly influences our lives, it can affect our minds and bodies. When stress indirectly influences our lives, it can also prompt maladaptive behaviors, such as bad eating habits, drug use, and the like.

Scientists, of course, recognize that stress is a leading cause of illness. In fact, about 70 to 80 percent of diseases are either caused by or affected by stress directly, such as somatoform diseases, depression, gastric ulcer disease, thyroid disease, endocrinologic disorders, and the like.

Stress greatly affects the nervous system, endocrine system, and immune system. High levels of stress also interfere with cognitive abilities, such as attention, concentration, and memory. High levels of stress also cause health problems in the form of headaches, muscle contractions, pupil dilations, bronchoconstrictions, chest pain, high blood pressure, and digestive problems, as well as, in some cases, sudden death.

Stress is cumulative and thereby can cause chronic distress. It is also acculturative, meaning that it may be experienced differently based on culture. In Western cultures, such as in North

America and Europe, human beings face challenges and goals individually, which is often more stressful. On the other hand, in collectivistic Eastern cultures, as in China and Japan, human beings face stress as a group, which can result in less stress and better stress management.

The definition of stress is elusive. To professionals in the field, stress is a negative emotional state that occurs as a response to an event that is being perceived by a living organism, including humans or animals, as taxing or exceeding that person's or organism's coping ability. In fact, such a stressor is perceived as a threat to psychological or physical well-being.

In scientific studies and treatment therapies, stress treatment is always a great concern for therapists. Specifically, therapists are focused on preventing stress and reducing stress.

The two scientists to first focus on stress and its consequences were Walter Cannon and Hans Seyle. Both Cannon and Seyle lived at the beginning of the nineteenth century.

Walter Cannon first detected the initial reaction to stress as the fight-or-flight response. It is a physiological reaction that occurs in response to a perceived harmful event (an attack or other threat to survival). Such a response primes the body to prepare for either a fight or flight. In women, stress can also create a tend-and-befriend response, which means seeking the protection of a social group in response to stressors. Given their need to handle childbirth, women also have more oxytocin hormone, which, among other things, creates a calming effect when they are faced with stressors.

Walter Cannon also detected that our endocrine system was involved in our reaction to stress. He further realized that individuals suffer from the consequences of distress, which can affect one's internal physiological balance and cause disease.

Hans Seyle, a Hungarian endocrinologist, studied the ideas of Walter Cannon, as well as those of Claude Bernard. Later, he reconceptualized their ideas with his own experiences. Seyle came up with the concept of the general adaptation syndrome, which analyzes a person's reaction to stress phenomena, as well as the "noxious agent," later referred to as stress, that creates such negative effects in that person. The world adopted Seyle's theories.

Hans Seyle detected that a person's glands and hormones are directly involved in the reaction to, and in the relief from, stress. He called positive stress *eustress* and negative stress *distress*.

Seyle stated that stress has three major stages, specifically, the alarm stage, the resistance stage, and the exhaustion stage.

First, the alarm stage is triggered when the organism perceives a stressor and the body reacts with a fight-or-flight response. The sympathetic nervous system is stimulated as the body's resources are mobilized to meet the threat or danger.

Second, during the resistance stage, the body resists and compensates as the parasympathetic nervous system attempts to return many physiological functions to their normal levels, while the body focuses resources against the stressor and remains on alert.

Lastly, if the stressor or stressors continue beyond the body's capacity, the resources become exhausted, and the body is susceptible to disease and death.

To cure and prevent the negative effects associated with stress is one of the main concerns of therapies. Indeed, it is important for the body to balance its homeostasis through metabolism, as well as to develop an adaptive mind, which is an important basis for good physical health.

Abraham Maslov's hierarchy of needs and self-actualization studies represented a humanistic approach to stress relief. He recognized that individuals have a happier and better balanced life through self-actualization and satisfaction of their needs. People with higher self-esteem and in better physical shape normally experience stress less severely. The elderly, children, and less adaptive people are more vulnerable to stress. Most importantly, a positive attitude, socializing, exercising, good physical health, and humor all can help a person to overcome and cope with stress.

On the other hand, some of the chronic stressors are poverty, exposure to crime, highly demanding jobs, tragic family events, natural disasters, unemployment, and the like.

Following World War II, scientists observed that many children died because they could not cope with the loss of their parents and with their new lives in orphanages. Psychologists also recognized that individuals, following a major disaster or catastrophe, suffer more anxiety and depression, post-traumatic stress disorder, and the like, with some consuming more drugs or alcohol. This is what happened to many survivors following September 11, 2001.

Psychologists measure stress, especially chronic stress, since it is a precursor for disease. An immediate study of stress is to measure a person's immediate physiological reaction to a stressor. One of the in-depth methods to measure stress is through undertaking a stress inventory, or stress journal, to see the subject's stress duration, magnitude, and onset. Treatment specialists more typically observe stress through an individual's daily activities.

During the nineteenth century, some psychologists more often used the Social Readjustment Rating Scale, but this did not show good predictors to mental and physical health. It did not consider a person's cognitive appraisal and coping ability. On the other hand, Richard Lazarus's study emphasized the importance of cognitive appraisal and coping ability. *Less ability for coping creates a higher stress level.*

So what can we do to prevent or reduce stress?

First, a person's positive appraisal and proper coping help. For example, living within our comfort zone and using humor can help. Second, avoiding or delaying a problem or conflict also helps to reduce distress. In particular, avoiding irritating events, engaging in joyful activities (such as the pursuit of our hobbies, music, exercise, and the like), and creating a peaceful and positive environment are beneficial. Lastly, utilizing our social (and in some cases, professional) support network can also help.

Our coping can be passive and defensive. Passive coping involves relaxation, meditation, rhythmical slow breathing, guided imagery, and disengagement. These coping activities also can be called quick relaxation techniques.

We might mask or shield our real-life problems, but this is only good to win time. Such defensive coping is a common defense mechanism.

This was first recognized by Sigmund Freud, the father of psychoanalysis, in the nineteenth century. Many of his theories are still used today. He explained that human beings maintain a level of instinctual tension among their various internal drives, all of which is mediated by their ego continuously.

Freud theorized that there is a conflict between our id (unconscious base desires) and superego (higher level of consciousness). The ego (our realistic self) is the intermediary that tries to resolve these conflicts between the id and superego before the next developmental stage occurs in an individual's life. Most importantly, where the conflict remains, it causes anxiety. In those cases where such anxiety is not relieved over the long term, it can cause disorders.

To avoid such negative outcomes, the ego distorts the mind by using its ego defense mechanism. The intent of ego is to relieve the mind and create inner peace. Such common defense mechanisms include repression, regression, denial, displacement, rationalization, projection, and sublimation.

Many of these terms are often used in popular culture as well. Some, however, require an explanation.

Regression means that an individual's personality reverts to an earlier stage of development, adopting more childish mannerisms, to avoid stress. Displacement means that the mind substitutes either a new aim or a new object for goals it felt in their original form to be dangerous or unacceptable. Sublimation is where socially unacceptable impulses or idealizations are unconsciously transformed into socially acceptable actions or behaviors. All these processes often occur at the subconscious level, where the individual is not even aware that he or she is engaging in such stress avoidance.

In more severe cases, psychotherapy and drug therapies are important, but just as important are an individual's positive appraisal and coping skills.

In conclusion, self-awareness, tolerance, a positive attitude, a sense of humor, and a healthy lifestyle, including exercise, are common prerequisites to avoiding and eliminating stress. It is also important to follow the Golden Rule in human relationships and to have a sense of humor in our daily lives. Societies also have to help their members by creating a healthier environment within which they can exist.

Printed in the United States
By Bookmasters